Separations

Separations

The Fiction Desk Anthology Series
Volume Ten

Edited by Rob Redman

The Fiction Desk

First published in 2016 by The Fiction Desk Ltd.

ISBN 978-0-9927547-6-1

Please note that we do not accept postal submissions.
See our website for submissions information.

www.thefictiondesk.com

The Fiction Desk Ltd
Registered in the UK, no 07410083
Registered office: Suite 1 First Floor, 41 Chalton Street, London, NW1 1JD

Printed and bound in the UK by TJ International, Cornwall.

Contents

Contents

Introduction

Rob Redman

It's easy to get caught up in the moment.

Like the author who drafts a novel in 1997, tweaks it in 2006, and then sits on it for a decade before publishing it to thunderous applause for having so perceptively observed and recorded the spirit of 2016, the zeitgeist is as much a hunting spirit as a hunted one.

And so this collection of stories, despite having come together over the last year or so, from writers around the globe, finds itself concerned with themes that are very much on our minds here and now.

As I write this introduction, the United Kingdom has just voted to leave the European Union. In response, Scotland is once again seriously discussing independence from the UK, and other countries around Europe are beginning to talk about the future of the EU as a whole, whether it is still viable, and which nations might follow the British example.

We don't know yet which (if any) of these various separations might take place, let alone what the ramifications might be. But as this anthology is prepared for press, it's hard not to notice that the following stories are very much concerned with the themes of union and separation. People move on; they die; gaps open up between where they mean to be and where they are; collaborations end.

The next months and years will be interesting and uncertain in Britain, in Europe, and across the world, and it's likely that most of us will be paying more attention to the news than usual, renewing old subscriptions or (the modern equivalent) downloading new apps. The following stories serve as a reminder that fiction too provides some of the tools we need to intrepret the world around us, our certainties and uncertainties, our hopes and despairs, our unifications and our separations.

Our first story examines the bonds that form between ourselves and the places where we live, how those places shape us, and how those bonds might continue to exist even after we're gone.

Alex Clark is gaining a reputation for stories that use the supernatural to explore our relationship with buildings: see also 'The Stamp Works' in our anthology There Was Once a Place. 'Poor Billy' won third prize in our 2015 Ghost Story Competition.

Poor Billy

Alex Clark

I live in a council flat.

There. I've said it. Take a moment to cover your surprise. Because if you were to look at me and guess where I belong, you'd probably imagine a villa. Yellow brick. Wisteria. A well-behaved Labrador, a broadsheet food section lying open on the kitchen table, Radio Four playing in the background. These things go very well with a neat blonde bob, with well-tailored trousers and quietly expensive shoes; they go very well with a job as a solicitor. They make sense. They work. And you'd be right, to an extent, because the flat's only a temporary home, but still: for now, I live in Brigham House.

Brigham House does not work with a neat blonde bob, well-tailored trousers, and quietly expensive shoes. In Brigham House,

I look like a social worker. I could be a GP on a home visit or, at a push, someone from the council. I do not live here. Brigham House is not the kind of place where people like me live. Brigham House is the kind of place that people like me think is inhabited by thugs and refugees, the kind of place where Staffordshire bull terriers roam the corridors and every lift stinks of pee.

That's nonsense, of course, but the place certainly looks bad from the outside. The House is not a house at all but a four-storey concrete box. It knows nothing of wisteria. It knows nothing of Labradors. It knows nothing of Staffordshire bull terriers either, because pets aren't allowed. There wouldn't be enough outdoor space for them anyway; just the poky dark 'balcony' that most tenants have filled with dead pot plants and broken-down bicycles. There's no garden, only some scrubby grass and a long concrete access ramp up to the main door.

The satellite dishes and the dribbly stains on the concrete are the only clues that anything's changed since it was built in the 1960s. One of four blocks in our little town (Joseph House, Oliver House, Brigham House, and Hyrum House), it was conceived and named by a Mormon councillor who was kicked out of office in 1968 after he was discovered to have quietly removed five thousand pounds of government money to fund his second family. The scandal distracted from the building work, meaning that although lifts were installed in Joseph, Oliver, and Hyrum Houses, Brigham House has only ever had an empty lift shaft. In 1993 they were going to pull it down anyway, so why bother; in 2000 they'd have it done in a year; ten years later nobody's got any money any more. And so in 2012 my newly wheelchair-bound mother, seventy-three years old and stubborn as a wine stain, gave in and announced she needed my help.

She's lived in the House for twenty years. Dad died twenty-one years ago, when I'd just left university, and as their council bungalow was then too big, Mum was relocated to a flat in Brigham House. Visiting her for the first time I was horrified, but once I got inside I could see it was fine, really, just not very pretty. As far as my mother was concerned, it was better than fine. She made friends; and, as she told me later in life, I should be keeping my money for my children, not spending it on an old lady who was perfectly happy where she was.

When you open the door to Brigham House, here's what you see: a long, grey, clean hallway, bare concrete for the walls and floor, a little rank of postboxes on your right. The shuttered opening for the non-existent lift is beyond them, and to your left is the cave beneath the stairwell, occupied by a forlorn pram and a racing bicycle with one wheel.

The stairs, with their dark blue handrail, rise to the first floor, turn back on themselves, rise again. On every floor the contents of the under-stair cave are familiar and as standard as if detailed by council rules: the first floor cave is old weightlifting kit, the second houses an ironing board, the third a collection of old plant pots and a milk crate. The fourth floor, where my mother lives, is the only one without a cubbyhole, meaning its tenants have to live tidier lives than those below.

I'm taking a breather at the top of the stairs with my mother's shopping when I see the flash of colour again.

I started to notice it a few weeks ago. I was out on the landing, having one of the cigarettes my mother doesn't know I still smoke. I'd like to say I don't make a habit of smoking in the building, but when it's raining and I've got to go four flights of stairs down and four back up afterwards, it doesn't seem like such a terrible thing to be doing. The windows on the stairwell are the slatted glass kind that never really close, so I tell myself it's well ventilated and I'm not doing any harm.

I was bending down to the floor, grinding the spark out on the sole of my shoe, when something red ran across the floor below. I say ran, but all I saw was the colour. Just a red flash, no noise, no fuss.

If I had been asked, I would have said it was a child. But there are no children in Brigham House; at least, not the small kind that run about hallways. On the ground floor someone has a baby, and on the second, a harassed woman named Janine has twin teenage boys. It could have been a cat of course, but remember: no pets allowed.

The second couple of times it happened I poked my head over the bannister, and the third I actually went down and had a look around. There was never anything there. And so now, when I see something strobe red through the gridded bars of the metal uprights, I begin to wonder if I don't have some terrible brain condition. This is ridiculous, but I am a woman of a certain age, and it's a similar age to the one at which my father dropped dead of an aneurysm.

I let myself into the flat, and am instantly comforted. Here is all the paraphernalia of my childhood memories: the ugly dark-wood hallstand, the pictures of sailboats in their silver frames, the little mirror that was my grandmother's. My mother is in the kitchen, boiling the kettle which I've moved to a little low table for her.

'Oh, Maggie,' she says, turning quickly, 'you gave me such a shock. You should knock when you come in. I can't hear you, you know.'

'I'm sorry, Mum,' I say, and fetch her the milk from the fridge.

'That's all right, love,' she says. 'Did you get everything?'

'Yes, it was fine,' I say, and find my eye caught by my father's gaze, coming at me from thirty years ago out of the family portrait hanging on the wall.

'Mum,' I say, impulsively, 'did Dad ever say anything to you about seeing things? Before he died?'

'No,' she says, frowning. 'I don't think so. Why?'

'Nothing, really. I just — I keep thinking I can see something in the hallway, on the stairs. Something red. I suppose there's a good explanation for it.'

'Oh, that's just Billy,' she says calmly, stirring the sugar into her tea. 'Poor Billy.'

I'm unloading the things from the shopping bags, but this is so baffling that I stop with the fridge door open and say, 'What?'

'Shut the fridge door, love,' she says. 'You're wasting electricity. It was just Billy, that's all.'

'Who's Billy?'

'He used to live here,' she says, her eyes looking upwards as she recalls the past. 'Oh, it was all very sad.'

I give up at this, close the fridge door and put the rest of the food on the kitchen counter. The kettle's just boiled, so I take down a mug for myself and plonk in a teaspoon of coffee, some hot water, and some sugar. In one of the bags there is a packet of biscuits, and I locate them before taking them through to the living room with my mother and asking her to tell me what exactly she is talking about.

'He was Freda's,' she says. 'She lived on three. Just by the stairs, where the Prestons live now. He was a sweet little thing, really, but she was trouble. Always drinking, and so many men coming round all the time. Selling herself, you know.'

'I don't remember any of this,' I say, shocked.

'Well, it was when I very first moved in. She was striking, very tall and blonde, and a good figure, but she always had a nasty look on her. Billy got shoved outside most of the day, so he didn't get in the way of her callers. 'Go and play,' she'd say, and then she'd lock him out. He was only about five. No lunch, poor thing. I used to let him in here to watch television, and give him a bit of food. He was always hungry.'

She dips the biscuit into her tea meditatively, and brings the softened edge up to her mouth. I'm struck once again by how kind she is, this woman who raised me, and I remember why I came here, to liftless, chilly, uncanny Brigham House.

'What happened to him?' I ask.

'I don't know,' she says simply. 'One day they were here, and the next they were gone. I thought the council had thrown them out because of what she did in the flat, but really, anything could have happened to them. It wasn't long after that that I started noticing Billy in the hallway. Just out of the corner of my eye, you know? Red. He always wore a little red coat.'

'You mean he's still here?' I say, frowning.

'Oh, not completely,' she says, calmly brushing the crumbs from her chin. 'Just a snatch of him, I think. Because do you know, when I went down to look for him there was never anyone there.'

'I didn't think your mum was the ghost type,' says my husband later, over the phone. I'm standing outside Brigham House, wrapped in my thin overcoat, holding a cigarette out of the wind.

'She isn't,' I say. 'That's why it's all so strange. I'm not even really sure that she meant a ghost. She said it was "just a snatch of him", as if he were a tune or a sentence.'

'She's going batty,' he says. Teasing me.

'She's not. She's sharp as a knife.'

'I miss you, you know,' he says, wistfully.

'I miss you too,' I say. 'You know I'll be home soon. When Peter comes over. He's booked his flights, he emailed me yesterday.'

'I can't believe your brother's actually taking responsibility,' he says, and I secretly agree, though I defend him to the hilt, of course. It's hard to believe that Peter is coming all the way from Vancouver to spend a month carting groceries up the stairs of Brigham House, but he is, and when he's here I can go back to my own home and my lovely husband.

'Are you sure you can't persuade her to move?'

'She says she's too old to bother moving everything, and that the physio told her she'd be up and about again in a couple of months. They offered her an accessible place, and she's turned it down. You know what she's like.'

'You should go,' he says, two hundred miles distant. 'You shouldn't be standing around the steps of a council block with a mobile phone. You're a sitting duck for muggers.'

'Don't be ridiculous,' I say, and, 'I love you.'

'I love you too,' he says, and I break off to cough, and he says, 'And I wish you'd give those things up.'

As I walk back up the stairs, wheezing gently, the metal doors to the lift shaft seem to watch me go.

The following week the British summer truly gets under way, with a series of gigantic thunderstorms. I spend all day in the flat watching the view from the windows come and go as fat drops pour from the sky, and when I get cabin fever I go and sit in floor three's cave and have a smoke.

The cave's milk crate comes in handy. If I take my overcoat off I can fold it over and over to make a pad for my bum, so that it doesn't get imprinted by the raised plastic edges. In the cave I feel like a naughty schoolgirl smoking in the toilets, and I find it strangely entertaining. People rarely come up the stairs – there are only eight flats on floors three and four, and bar my mother they all go to work – but I have a plan about what I will do if discovery threatens. I will pretend to be tidying up. A middle-aged woman can be largely invisible when she wants to be; or, frankly, even when she doesn't. But I never need to put the plan into action, because my hours in the hallway are entirely solitary.

As so often happens when you are entirely solitary, after a while I begin to talk to myself.

'Billy, Billy, Billy,' I murmur. 'Hmmm.' I wonder what it must have been like for him, poor Billy. The door that used to be his mother's is over there, freshly painted blue, innocent and blank as a new-made leaf. I put my feet up on the plant pot and take a long draw. 'I wonder where you are now?'

Though I can't quite bring myself to believe in him, I find myself talking to Poor Billy more as the week goes on. 'You know,' I say, letting a long breath out, 'I'm not sure that ghosts exist.'

He doesn't have much to say to this.

'If they did,' I add, 'I think my dad would have come back, don't you?'

He doesn't have anything to say to that, either.

'Because ghosts have always died suddenly, haven't they? And unexpectedly. And that fits.'

I shift on the milk crate, because even through the coat it's not the most comfortable seat. 'It was a brain aneurysm, you know. At least it was quick.' Absurdly, I turn my face away from his door as I say this because I know I'm not telling Billy the whole truth. I haven't told him that my father smoked two packs of cigarettes a day, or what 'significant contributory factor' means. But he's probably too young to understand anyway. Especially when he doesn't exist.

'Anyway,' I continue, 'if you're going to be a ghost, you should really have a message. Ghosts usually do. Something important they have to say.'

At the other end of the hallway, the blocked-up lift shaft looks at me. The corner of one of the metal shutters has been dented, probably by a delivery man, and a tiny triangle of black is visible behind it. Although I know it's ridiculous, I don't like it. I've never liked doors with dark behind them. Attic hatches in bedroom ceilings bother me, unless they're the kind with bolts underneath. I can't sleep knowing there's a black hole above me, not unless I know the dark's been firmly locked out.

I get up and scoot one of the plant pots across the hallway with my foot, so that it stands in front of the little triangular opening. I'll have to move it back when I'm finished, but for now it comforts me.

As I turn to go back to my smoking den, in my peripheral vision a flash of red crosses the hallway and is gone. I stand for a minute, the smoke from my cigarette drifting upwards in the gentle breeze.

The end of the week brings my mother's appointment with the physiotherapist. At seven a.m. on the day of the appointment, having been sitting drinking tea since waking from a wheelchair-related nightmare at four, I decide I can't face trying to get her down the stairs on my own. I'll have to get help.

I go out into the hallway and listen. Our floor is silent, but somewhere on the third is the sound of a radio. It's coming from the door I think of as Poor Billy's flat.

It's Mr Preston who answers my knock; a squat, cheerful man whose frame doesn't look big enough to support his gut. 'Old Ellie?' he says, after he's turned the radio down. 'Oh yeah, no problem. Lovely lady. You're her daughter, are you? Just give me a minute.'

It turns out he does removals for a living, so he's used to carrying awkward weights. We bump my mother down the stairs and wheel the chair out to the waiting taxi, I ask her yet again to give me a ring once she's safely at the hospital, and she tells me to stop fussing.

As the cab drives away, Mr Preston holds his hand out to me and says 'Stu, by the way. Just give me a shout if you need help again.'

We walk back to Brigham House, and in the hallway he pauses at the bottom before starting the long climb up. He pats his side contemplatively and says, 'I should lose some weight, really. Too many cooked lunches, that's what does it.'

'Well, I should probably give up smoking,' I say.

'Yeah, I might want to think about that as well,' he says. 'There was someone asking after your mum yesterday evening, by the way. Didn't want to say in front of her.'

'Why not?' I say, puzzled.

He screws his face up and raises his hand in a vague gesture. 'Well... he looked like police, if you ask me. Black chap, nice suit, posh voice. Asking about some kid who used to live here.'

'Billy,' I say, and my eyes rise to the railings above. There's nothing there. There never is when you're looking straight at it.

'That's the one,' says Stu. 'Kid used to live in our flat, apparently. The bloke asked if anyone was still here from that time, and when I said your mum's name he got quite excited and said he wanted to talk to her. I just said she wasn't in. I don't know, it's just — I'm a law-abiding man, but I always think you don't want to be telling the police any more than you have to, if you know what I mean.'

'Fair enough,' I say, though truthfully I don't understand the attitude. Still, Stu is a nice man, and I'm not about to start questioning his views. 'Thank you.'

'No problem.'

When the doorbell rings an hour later, I find myself face to face with a young black man in a smart suit. He is handsome, with deep-set regular features and a pleasant smile. 'Sorry to bother you,' he says politely, 'but are you Mrs Henson's daughter? I'm hoping to speak to her.'

'Yes, I'm her daughter, but I'm afraid she's out,' I say. 'Can I help?'

He looks disappointed. 'I've missed her again. Perhaps I could come back tomorrow?'

'Of course,' I say, burning with curiosity. 'Shall I tell her you called?'

'She won't know my name,' he says apologetically. 'But here, let me give you a card,' – he produces his wallet and rifles through – 'with my number on it, just in case another time would be better.' The card he proffers is for Sidgwick Barret Price, Architects. 'That's me,' he says, indicating the name at the bottom of the card: Matthew Brunswick.

'What was it you wanted to talk to her about, if you don't mind me asking?'

He looks faintly embarrassed, as if there's something he doesn't want to say to me. 'Nothing important really, I'm just interested in someone who used to live here. Someone I have a connection to. It was a long time ago, but I'd just like to talk to someone who might remember.'

'I see,' I say. 'Well, if you want to come back tomorrow, we'll be in most of the day.'

'Thank you very much,' he says. 'I'll see you then.'

I stand in the door seeing him out, and I notice that as he walks along the hallway he reaches out a thin, elegant hand and allows his fingertips to brush against the bare concrete of the wall. It is a strange gesture, gentle and oddly personal. He might be stroking a human face, or a lover's hand. It makes me feel voyeuristic, standing there staring at his retreating back, and I get a grip on myself and close the door.

Mum comes back at half past nine, and the taxi driver volunteers to help us back up the stairs. She is baffled by the news of the visitor. 'Brunswick,' she says. 'Brunswick. No, I don't know anyone called that. I suppose we'll find out what it is tomorrow.'

Once we've got Mum indoors and I've gone out to thank the taxi driver and see him back down, I stand for a while leaning over the bannisters. Behind me, the front door of the flat opens awkwardly, and my mother manoeuvres herself out. 'Are you going to be long, Mags?' she says. 'Only I could do with some help in the bathroom.'

'No Mum,' I say. 'Just coming.'

'Are you all right?' she says. 'You look like you're fretting about something.'

'I'm okay,' I say. 'I was just thinking — you don't suppose, do you Mum, that something bad happened to Billy?'

'Billy?' she says. 'Sweetheart, that was an awfully long time ago. Maybe I wish I could have done more, but there's no point dwelling on it now.'

'You're right,' I say, and I turn and smile at her. As I meet her gaze, her eyes flicker just a fraction to the left, and she makes a little noise like a small 'Oh —'

'What is it?' I say, looking round.

'Nothing, love,' she says. 'Come inside.'

The ring on the doorbell comes at eight the next morning, when I'm spreading peanut butter on my toast. My mother wakes at six every day, in response to the early-morning call of old age, so I'm washed and dressed by seven. It's a bit early to be knocking, even so, and I'm scowling as I open the door. It's him again.

'I'm sorry to disturb you so early,' he says. 'It's just that I have to go to work, and I'd really love to have a chat with Mrs H.'

At which point my mother turns the corner into the hall to see what's going on, stops, screws her eyes up in disbelief, and says loudly, 'Billy?'

'Mrs Henson!' he says, and his face, which I see now is a kind of pale creamy brown with even, generous features, the kind of face you get when your father is a handsome black man and your mother a striking blonde, breaks into a broad smile, and he holds his hands out towards my mother and walks forward into our hallway.

So nothing bad happened to Billy. The lift shafts are empty, the stairwells unhaunted. Billy's here on our sofa, drinking tea with my mother and telling her about his adoption.

'It was difficult,' he says. 'I didn't understand why I couldn't see my mum, and I couldn't go home. And I was freaked out by the fact they were black.' He waves a hand over his face. 'I know, I know, weird. But Mum was white, you see. And it took me ages to see why I was placed with them. But that was the policy. They were supposed to understand me more, and show me where I fitted in.'

'And where did you go?' says my mother, eyes shining, wanting to know all about it. 'Was it near here?'

'No, no,' he says. He names a city a good fifty miles away. 'We had a house,' he says, smiling. 'A garden and everything. I loved it, once I got used to it. And they loved me. I was their only one. When I was twelve I decided I was going to be an architect, and that was it. They supported me all the way through university.' He laughs reflectively. 'I was probably a bit spoilt. But I was very happy.'

'Oh, I'm so glad,' says my mother, reaching out and clasping her papery hand over his. 'I thought of you often, you know. I felt so sorry for you. You were such a sad little mite.'

'Yes and no,' he says reflectively, looking upwards. 'Things at home weren't good, but I really loved this place.'

'Really?' I blurt out, surprised. 'But you were so small, and being left to run around the hallways on your own...' I tail off, aware that I sound judgemental.

'Exactly!' he says, laughing. 'To a five-year-old, this building's an adventure kingdom. I used to spend so long sitting on an old milk crate under the stairs.'

'It's still there,' I say.

'No!' he says, delighted. 'That was my special lair. Man, I was so many things in there. I had this red coat, and I'd put just the hood of it over my head and run up and down the hall being Superman.' He shakes his head, smiling. 'I made up my own code and spent hours keeping a secret diary about nothing, really. And then I'd go round to Mrs H's when I got hungry, and she'd give me soup and biscuits.'

'But you always looked so sad,' says my mother, confused, still holding his fingers in her little paw.

'Oh, don't get me wrong,' he says, and behind the bland phrase I feel a tendril of darkness reach out and pass over the sun. 'The evenings were bad. But out there, I could be anything I wanted. Sometimes I think that's why I became an architect.'

'And what do you build?' I ask, pouring us some more tea.

'Not much at the moment,' he says. 'I'm still training. But I want to specialise in concrete.'

My mother makes a face. 'Like this place?' she says. 'It's all right, but it's a bit ugly, isn't it?'

'Oh no,' he says, and I can tell from the way his face lights up that we're talking about his passion now. 'I mean yes, it's not traditionally beautiful. But it has the most fantastic properties. It absorbs all kinds of things. Sound, for instance — not impact sound, you know, sharp sounds, but just the sound of day-to-day life — and heat, it absorbs heat too, but slowly, gradually, and then later when the temperature drops it slowly gives it back out.' He looks at our faces, and laughs. 'But I'm boring you.'

'Not at all,' says my mother. 'I'm so glad you came round.'

'I just wanted to meet someone who knew me when I was Billy,' he says. 'It's taken me so long to come back here, but I always meant to. It sounds weird, I know, but I always felt like I left a little bit of myself here.'

He shakes his head as if shaking off a dream, glances at his watch and sucks his breath in. 'I'm so sorry,' he says, 'but I've got to go. I've got a meeting in half an hour.'

'Will you come back?' says my mother. 'I'd love to chat again. I could make you some soup.'

'That sounds perfect, Mrs H,' he says, getting up. 'And I should say thank you, as well, for all the times you were kind to me when I was here. I really appreciate it.'

'Oh, it was no problem,' she says, trying to hide her pleasure.

'I'll show you out,' I say. 'Don't worry, Mum.' I pick up my coat on the way past, with the secret packet of cigarettes in the inside pocket.

In the hallway, I can see my chance leaving. I wait until we're in the concrete kingdom of the stairwell, and in a rush I say, 'Did you feel like you had to come back here for a reason?'

'Excuse me?' he says.

'There wasn't anything you felt like you had to say?' I ask hurriedly. 'Like a message.'

He looks at me, as if alerted to something, and for a moment we meet each other's gaze in silence. I expect him to ask me what I'm going on about, but eventually, as if he has recognised something curious and unexpected in me, he says, 'I don't think so.'

'So you don't have any kind of message,' I say, prepared to push it just a bit, just in case.

He looks across at me, raises his eyebrows and shrugs. As we cross the hallway the chill from the always-slightly-open louvres hits me and I swing the coat round my shoulders. I miss the sleeve, and as I feel around for it the cigarette packet falls out of my pocket and onto the floor. Billy bends and picks it up. As he hands it back to me, he says, 'I've got a message.'

'What is it?' I say, shaking a cylinder out of the pack as we pass the lift shaft doors and start the long descent down the stairs.

'You should give those up,' he says, and winks.

I look at the pack in my hand, with its single bony finger reaching forward for mine, and I know he's right. I press the cylinder back among its fellows and pocket the box as we turn the corner onto the next set of stairs, the sound of our footsteps bouncing and clattering around us, echoing between the concrete walls and lasting long after we are gone.

The first of several stories in the current volume that deal with the loss of a loved one, Hannah Mathewson's story asks how we reconcile our responsibilities to ourselves, to our families, and to the wider world, when the lights go out.

Two Pounds, Six Ounces

Hannah Mathewson

I think I saw the lights flicker as I drove into the car park, but at the time I thought it was lightning. Stupid, really. It was a flash of darkness, the exact opposite of lightning, but I was fumbling with the heater, trying to blast some hot air into my clothes before I step back into the rain, and I wasn't really looking.

I call my brother but he doesn't pick up. I don't want to go in alone, and the storm is keeping me in the car anyway, but it's too terrible just to sit here, so I get out and run for the entrance. In the time it takes to cross the car park, the rain has soaked my hair and is trickling down my neck, and I can feel it freshly penetrating my shoes. There's a wide puddle in front of the doors, but when you're as wet as you can be it doesn't matter anyway, so I run through it.

David's not in the foyer. If he had arrived already, this is where he'd be, because all these hospital corridors look the same and he knows I can never find Mum's room. It's no help that they've moved her so many times. I learned the route to intensive care the day they moved her to recovery. Then there was the day I found her new room by myself and it was empty: Mum had been rushed to surgery again. Since then I've been having dreams about arriving in vacated hospital rooms, with beds made up and flowers disposed of, and I'm afraid to go looking for her on my own.

The wind is rattling the glass and throwing pulpy leaves across the vinyl every time the doors open. I try David again but there's still no answer. The weather was half this bad the day of the accident, but that's how I know he'll be driving carefully. I tell myself I'm not worried. There's a ladies' bathroom just past the stairs and I go there to dry off. As I'm tousling my hair under the hand dryer the lights flicker again and the dryer cuts out. I get it to turn on again, but it makes me wonder what happens to Mum if the powers goes. Suddenly I don't want to wait for David anymore and I go back into the corridor. Two men with staff badges on their lapels are escorting an electrician towards the east wing. I know he's an electrician because he did the restaurant a few months ago when we blew a fuse. His name's Robin. Maybe I'm being suspicious, but I think they might be in a hurry. One of the men is leading Robin by the elbow.

I pass the gift shop, and I pause and think about buying Mum flowers one last time. It's even more pointless than usual. She's been unconscious since the accident, but at least before she might have woken up and seen them. Now I would probably just be taking them home again.

I find the staircase I think will take me to Mum's ward, but this is the biggest hospital in four hundred miles and I'm not sure. Maybe her last room was this way. Maybe I'm on the wrong side of the building. As I take the stairs I hear hurried feet above, and voices.

'This just can't happen.'

'It might not.'

Two doctors, a man and a woman, come around the corner and start when they see me. The woman smiles weakly and they carry on past. I stand and listen to them go, but they're talking in hushed tones now and I can't hear.

I come out on the second floor and go to the window. The branches of a birch are being battered against the glass. I look across the courtyard, and even through the downpour I'm sure I recognise the ostentatious vase of purple orchids in a window opposite. They're the ones Auntie Connie sent. I'm not where I thought I was.

I take a left, thinking I can circle the courtyard and come out on the right ward, but I find myself on the paediatric floor. Phones seem to be ringing everywhere. Two men in scrubs pass by, and I hear one of them say the fire service is being summoned. I think I see the lights flicker again but I'm not sure if it's my imagination. There's an awful creak as a strong wind hits the near side of the building, and all around me, tiny patients start up a chorus of wailing. I try to get directions from a doctor but she tells me to go back to my child, to not panic.

I'm not panicking. I'm not feeling much of anything, except tired. Until four days ago I was pure anxiety and desperate hope. But then the deadline for improvement came and went, as we knew it would. Mum's doctor said he set the deadline for our benefit, for mine and David's. He said it was to help us believe we had done everything we could so we could let go. There wasn't any hope. There hadn't been for weeks.

There are two nurses sat at a desk in an alcove. I approach them and I'm about to ask for directions when I hear what they're saying.

'If the power goes, we're done for. We don't have the staff,' whispers the first. Her voice is breaking. She looks barely twenty.

'We can't panic. There's an engineer fixing the backup generator now.'

So that's the problem: no backup generator. As I head in what I hope is the right direction, I try calling David again. He must be here by now. I'll tell him not to wait in the foyer. I'll tell him to get to Mum. It's only ten past nine, and we weren't turning her off until ten. We'd decided ten for some reason, perhaps because it feels like bedtime. But if the power goes she'll die before then. I wonder if we should say goodbye and get it over with, so at least we'll be ready, but I know I won't suggest it. If there's no power cut we'll have thrown the last minutes of her life away. Every minute has been the same as the last for nine weeks now, but still.

There's no answer from David. I can only hope he's already at the room, because as I reach the end of the ward I realise I can't come this way, it's a dead end, and that's when the lights go out. Even though I know it won't, I wait for the backup generator to kick in. There's a beat of silence before people start to panic. From all corners of the blackened floor, murmurs turn to cries. The rain seems louder. Some of the staff produce medical torches, helpless specks of light to show them their own feet, and start stumbling for their patients. I wonder about all those life support machines in intensive care. I wonder about surgery.

I need to find Mum. If there are no lights, there's no life support, which means she's dying. I make contact with the wall and with a hand against it I start navigating my way back to the stairs. The emergency exit signs must lead that way so I follow them slowly back along the corridor. They seem to glow with increasing brightness but it's just my eyes adjusting. I can make out the windows too, but only just. Between the night and the driving rain, it's barely any lighter outside.

Some of the staff have proper torches now and are rushing by me to the paediatric floor, where someone's shrieking for help. I drown them out and keep on in the other direction. I reach the window by the stairs and I'm looking out across the courtyard again. The orchids are gone. Mum's room is dark. Or maybe I'm not where I thought I was. Maybe this is a different window. I think that's a birch tree outside, the courtyard is full of them, but it's blowing a different way now.

I can hear people shouting things I don't understand. Maybe the staff are getting organised and maybe they're panicking, I don't know. I think I've found the door to the staircase when two people with a torch rush by. They're talking about babies on ventilators and not enough hands to 'manually bag' them all, and I make a decision I will second-guess for the next hundred and forty-five minutes.

'I can help,' I hear myself say, and they lead me back the way I came and put me in a sterile gown. We go to a room full of cribs and stricken new parents. I'm brought to a baby with no one by it, and by torchlight I'm shown how to work a BVM, a mask attached to a bag I need to squeeze every three seconds. Gently, so the baby's stomach doesn't fill with air. And then I'm breathing for a three pound infant, and it's too late to be with Mum. At least David will be there by now.

There's a snap of lightning, it makes a sound like a whip right on top of us, and children are crying again in nearby rooms. I ask when the power will be back on but no one hears. The person with the torch moves on, teaching parents to ventilate their own tiny bundles of pink transparent skin, and

I'm left to work in darkness. Out in the hall, I hear wheels. Torches dragging trolleys and units keep passing by the door. I wonder if it's battery-operated equipment they're hauling around, and if they'll manage to save everyone. I wonder how much of it they have and how many patients will die without electricity.

No one will try and save Mum. Not when there are people worth saving. No one will be thinking about her except me and my brother. I want to call David again and make sure he's at the room but one hand is on the baby's head, holding the mask in place, and the other is squeezing every three seconds. I won't know until I get out of here whether my mother is dying alone. I wonder if I've done a stupid thing.

There are sirens outside as the fire service arrives. Someone tells us they're here to rig up emergency lights. I suddenly realise this will be on the news and it unnerves me for some reason. Maybe it's the idea of people knowing what I've done. Not that anyone would. Surgical staff trying to keep an open patient alive in perfect darkness is a story. A brain-dead woman fading away forty-five minutes early is not.

A fire engine's lights cut through the rain as it pulls up outside. We can see each other's faces, taut and pallid in the blue light. The only doctor with his hands free draws up the blinds, though they were open anyway and it makes little difference. He tells us the fire crew are rigging floodlights to the ladder. At an angle he can see a second truck doing the same. I wonder about the other rooms, Mum's room, facing the courtyard.

It takes a long time to raise the ladders because of the wind. A woman with a palm-size baby asks if the ladder might be blown into the building. I nearly say, 'Is this not enough of a disaster already?' but she looks so fragile, and even younger than I am.

She might be a teenager. Besides, the other parents seem panicky about the idea. I suppose the law of averages stops meaning much when your newborn child is on life support.

The fire crews raise their ladders without incident and the floodlights are switched on. They're shining from the full height of the building, another two storeys above, and to the left of us. The cold light throws harsh shapes across the room and fails to reach more than half of it, and everything in the beam looks like it's vibrating in the shadow of the rain, but it's still an improvement. It'll do.

I expect my baby to react to the light but it doesn't. I don't know whether it's sleeping or whether it's too small and frail to move. I suppose I wouldn't be here if its tiny body was working properly. Right in front of me, a card on the crib says 'Charlotte'. A little girl. She has a surgical scar running the length of her chest and she's practically wrapped in wires. There's one caught around her ankle. It might pull if she moves but I don't have a free hand to untangle her. I think I'd be afraid to touch her even if I could. If I had a baby this small and delicate I wouldn't let a stranger near her, let alone a stranger who would abandon her dying mother. I wouldn't let her leave her hospital crib until she could smile up at me and blink her eyes in the light.

A chart below her name tag is tracking her weight gain. Most days have a smiley face stamped next to them, which I guess means she's doing well, but when she was born, ten days ago, she weighed just two pounds, six ounces.

Two pounds, six ounces. They probably removed more than that of Mum the day of the accident. The parts of her bowel that were crushed by the steering wheel when the airbag failed. The circle of skull they cut out to get to her engorged brain. All that blood swilling around her abdomen. The paramedics said she was unconscious at the scene and she's never woken up. In a stupid way I'm glad, because she's never been in any pain. When I picture the accident, her head hits the windshield and she's gone like that, doesn't even know she's crashed.

At least I can hope she doesn't know, and I can hope she isn't in pain. Even if it means she hasn't caught a word of me begging her to try harder, and telling her I'm too young to lose my mum and too in love with her to bear it.

There's another roar of thunder overhead. It sounds like the building peeling apart, or being lifted from its foundations and taking off in the storm. I hold my breath and wait for us to keel to one side like a ship. There's a commotion along the ward. Whoever needed help is still wailing but it's a different kind of sound. I think maybe somebody's child has died, and before I know it I've stopped squeezing every three seconds and I don't know how long it's been. I panic and call for the doctor. It's alright, he tells me, I haven't done any harm, but for a moment while he's examining Charlotte the whole room goes still. It takes several minutes for the atmosphere of shock to dissipate, and I wonder how these people manage it, being responsible for something so helpless.

Not all the other babies have parents with them. One mother is ventilating a tiny bundle with bandages around its head while her partner cares for their own, and most of the others are with nurses. A nurse bagging the baby next to Charlotte asks who I am and I lie. I tell her I had a panic attack and came to the emergency room, but I'm alright now. Everyone's impressed that I offered to help and they all thank me and say kind things. I suppose I did the right thing, I just didn't know you could regret doing it, and I wonder if I will when all this is over. I wonder what David will say.

I ask the nurse about Charlotte's parents. She tells me they live an hour away and probably don't know about the power cut. They were here only this evening, like every other evening.

They're skittish, like most of the parents, because their last daughter was stillborn and Charlotte was delivered by emergency Caesarean. The nurse tells me they'll be beyond grateful that I'm keeping their daughter alive, but even this doesn't make me feel better.

Maybe an hour passes and the power doesn't come back on. The wailing from along the corridor stops. The wind continues to groan and the rain never lets up, but it still seems quiet. Just voices and the storm. I wonder if Mum's still breathing. I read online that sometimes people take hours to go after their life support is switched off, but somehow I don't think Mum is one of those people. That machine has been breathing for her for so long that I don't know if her body would remember how to do it alone.

I wish I could know for sure if it was over but since I can't, I find myself willing the power to stay off. It doesn't make much sense, but I'd rather get there an hour too late than five minutes. I suppose, really, I don't want to get there at all. Maybe that's what I'm doing here. I look down at little Charlotte and remind myself of her parents, of how she can't even open her eyes to the light. Okay, if I wasn't here maybe that doctor would be ventilating her, but then maybe some other kid would die instead. He keeps coming and going, he's probably the only mobile person on the ward. But I feel like I'm lying to myself, even though it's true, and I wish I could go back and unthink those things about avoiding seeing Mum die.

Now I feel like I've abandoned David as well. We were supposed to do this together, and now because of me he's alone in that room, doing the hardest thing with no one with him.

Or maybe he's not. Maybe the storm held him up. Or maybe he did what I did and is helping someone who might live. I flash back to the foyer, to the wet leaves on the vinyl. The automatic doors. Maybe he never even got into the building. I wonder if they can slide open those doors without power. I wonder if there's another way in.

I picture Mum again, slowly fading without her life support, only this time David isn't there. I wonder if anyone even checked on her when the power went. I wouldn't blame them if they didn't. There are maybe a dozen critically ill people on Mum's ward who would have needed help. Besides, David and I said we'd be there at nine. Does any part of the mush inside her battered skull know that it's dark and there's no one there?

There's a flash of lightning, and in my mind it lights up Mum's pale features, the useless breathing tube still stuck in her throat. It would have been removed when we turned her off, I guess so she could look peaceful when she died. If there's no one there, I suppose it doesn't matter. It's not like she can feel it. At least I don't think she can.

An hour stretches into two. I'm only getting calmer, but the parents are nervous. Without any heating, it's got cold fast, though I can't tell how cold because my clothes are still wet and it's making me shiver. The doctor is obsessing over the babies' vital signs and covering them in thermal blankets. The rain goes on and on and I think about that puddle by the entrance. It's probably seeping under the sliding doors by now. I think about calling Mum to remind her to close the basement window. I'm thinking it before I'm really thinking it, before I remember. The basement will be flooded. It's probably been flooded since the day of the accident. I called her that day to remind her to close it like I always do — did — in heavy rain, but she didn't pick up. She was driving.

I stop thinking about the basement. I'll need to check if it's flooded, but I don't want to think about being at that house after tonight, so I decide not to remember. Instead I think about whether the power cut has made the news already. Maybe Charlotte's parents are on their way, terrified for her life. I hope not. I don't want to meet them. I don't want anyone else to tell me I did something admirable when I'm not sure that I did. Besides, it's dangerous out there.

There isn't much conversation. Every so often someone speculates about the reach of the power cut, or what's happening in the operating theatres, or who's getting fired for this. Really, there's nothing to talk about, because no one knows. Then the doctor tells us he's worked in the Congo, in a clinic without the most basic equipment, so I guess this barely qualifies as a bad day at work for him. But I think the teenage mother is afraid of the dark and thunder. She even looks afraid of her kid. She'll probably have nightmares about this. And then there's me.

We get word that the backup generator is done for: it'll need to be replaced. It's too much for some of the parents. Their anxiety becomes anger and they start wondering aloud how this could happen, but the staff don't have any answers, and they're obviously not to blame, so their anger just sits in the air. I can't think of anything to say that won't make it worse so I just stand quietly, breathing it in. But in the end it doesn't matter, because ten minutes later the power comes back on, and just like that the darkness could have been a dream. It isn't even the same room any more. There's a mural on my right, the Very Hungry Caterpillar, that I can't quite believe has been there the whole time. I think I can hear the relief from all over the hospital, but it's just the hum of the lights. The storm seems quieter, further away.

Machines start beeping back to life and the staff go about hooking babies up to ventilators. I cast my eyes to the ground and pray that Charlotte and I can go unnoticed. I don't want to leave. I don't want to leave so badly that tears come to my eyes. If the power cut was a dream I'm very, very awake now, and if they take Charlotte off me I'll forget the dream altogether.

The doctor comes over to us, and when he sees I'm crying he puts a hand on my shoulder.

'It's all right. It's over now,' he tells me, and I start gasping for air. I can't see for crying, I can't hear anything but my own ragged sobs. Hands wrestle the BVM off me and I try to tell them no, don't take it, but I don't have any strength to resist. Everyone thinks I'm having another panic attack, and they tell me how brave I was to manage and how heroic I've been. I don't want to hear all that again, and it makes me pull myself together. The staff want to give me oxygen but I tell them no, I can breathe, I just want to clean myself up and go home. I need to get out of there after all.

I calm down enough to persuade them to let me go, but before I do I stand over Charlotte's crib again. I haven't had a proper look at her face and I still can't see it now. The mask has been replaced with a tube like Mum's. I lift her tiny pink foot with one finger and unwrap the wire from around her ankle. The limb's heavier than I think it will be, a dead weight, and I wish she would move just a bit so I know there's someone in there, but she doesn't. I put my little finger against her cheek. It's warm. It'll have to do.

I go all the way back to the foyer before I think it's safe to ask for directions. The man at the front desk is too helpful. I think he can tell I've been crying so he talks to me like a child. It makes me feel like a child, like I'm lost in the supermarket and looking for my mum. As I leave the desk I know exactly where I'm going, and it makes the tears come again because I'm all out of excuses.

As I reach the room, a nurse hurries over to me, and I know then that David isn't here. As she tells me how it's been perfect chaos, I notice she's on the verge of tears. They don't know how long Mum's been gone, she tells me. Probably since only minutes after the power went. The storm came suddenly. The generator was fine this morning. They just didn't have the staff.

She holds the door open for me and we go inside together. Someone's taken her breathing tube out but she still doesn't look like Mum. She's white already, all the blood has sunk away from her face, and when I take her hand she's cold too. Sometimes people say the dead look like they could be sleeping but Mum definitely isn't. The nurse offers to make me a cup of tea and I say yes even though I don't want one. Then Mum and I are alone. I don't know what to do, or say to her, so I sit away from the bed, against the wall, and stare at the purple orchids on the windowsill.

The rain goes on. With Mum's machines turned off it's the only sound in the room. I've never noticed other people breathing before but without the sound of it now I feel alone. A gust of wind hits the glass and I shiver.

Another nurse comes in and tells me he's seen David doing laps of the corridors, afraid to come to the room. A few minutes later he appears on a chair by the nurses' station with his head in his hands. I tell every staff member I can find that I'll be right back, that I'm only leaving Mum for a second, and I go and sit next to him. I tell him Mum's gone and he nods and wrings his hands. He was trapped in the elevator, twenty paces and half a floor away. Somehow he knew I wasn't at the room. He says he had a feeling I'd be helping some scared old man back to his bed or something, and for some reason that's when I know I did the right thing.

A senior staff member comes by to tell us what happened, but we know what happened. She offers us her condolences on behalf of the hospital and says she wishes they could have done more for Mum. We understand, we say. No, we won't be suing anyone.

We go to the room and sit either side of the bed, close to her slack, grey face. I press her cool fingers to my cheek and tell her I'm sorry, but I know she would understand. It's not like she was here anyway. Through his tears, David tells her that it's okay, that we're glad she's at peace, that we'll manage on our own.

After an interval, maybe over an hour, someone brings David the paperwork. He's her next of kin. He's the head of the family now. I feel a wave of sympathy as I watch him struggle to steady his hand and hold the pen straight. I wonder if he feels that same awful responsibility for me as I did for Charlotte. Mum must have felt it for us both, and it makes me wish I'd known it better when she was alive.

David suggests we go get a bottle of something strong and both stay the night at his place. But it's not easy to leave. We kiss her cheeks and squeeze her hands and cry like children into the bed sheets. David says leaving her here feels like failing her all over again, and I tell him we never failed her. We did everything we could.

We break our vigil, stretching and shaking our limbs as we stand like we can shed the grief that way. Then David takes my hand and marches us from the room. We don't look back, there's no use. He keeps up a brisk pace and I take twice as many steps to match him.

Outside the ward, a nurse is leading an elderly patient by the arm. She's telling him he was supposed to stay in bed, that she was worried he'd fallen in the dark. He didn't fall, he tells her. He sat with the woman in the coma, down the hall.

Maybe he means Mum. Maybe she wasn't alone after all. I think about speaking to him but I'm afraid I'm wrong. And anyway, David doesn't hear. With my hand in his, we keep walking.

Families are perhaps the groups in which togetherness can be the most insular, and separation lead to the most unpredictable outcomes. The following story won the 2016 Newcomer Prize.

Renaissance Man

James Mitchell

{gravity}

Pemberton and the rest of the faculty are always laughing at the half-a-paperweight on my desk, hiding it around my office or asking me to throw it away. But would you throw away, say, your child's first tooth? You might, for hygiene reasons, but I've filed down the sharper edges of this paperweight fragment so that nothing stands in the way of me treasuring Isaac's first achievement in the world of science. As it happens I threw out the tooth: it was exam season, and I wasn't thinking.

Isaac discovered Gravity at the age of two, just after Cutting Food Nicely but still before Inside Voice and Shoelaces. It was very cute. I say cute, and I mean it now, but at the time it was quite maddening. Hypothesis: parenting is the petri dish of nostalgia.

'Now George,' Marie had said, scrubbing rotten banana from her work shawl, 'this is what you wanted for the boy.'

'RAVITEE!' he'd cried from the upstairs landing, and his pudgy fingers had hurled the glass orb through the air. I remember it catching a beam of light through the thatched roof and refracting the inscription — TO GEORGE, FOR TEN YEARS OF TEACHING — into my eyes, before landing at my feet. Half of it shattered into glittering powder, and it took Marie and me until dusk to sweep it out of the hairs of the goatskin rug. Isaac sat on the rickety stairs the whole time and watched us, beaming like he'd woken up to snowfall. I smiled at him, as Marie and I had planned we would in situations like these, but he stared straight through me, his lips mouthing the three syllables of the force he'd just discovered.

Marie whispered in my ear: 'Why did you let it fall?'

As I plucked another grain of glass from the goatskin I wondered just that. For a moment I had reached out a hand to catch it, but that would've been messing with the data, contaminating the great Fair Test that was our little boy's childhood.

Around the demi-paperweight, my desk at the university reconfigures each term according to the workload of my students, shedding old coursework like dead skin, but two things never move. One is the family photo, a crumbly, sepia thing that looks exaggeratedly old in its stainless-steel frame. Pemberton assumes we got it done at the Past Tymes Period Photo stand in the shopping centre, and I have to let him. I'm standing there in my costume, and Marie leans back into me, her arms tucked into a brown pinny. Isaac, then nine, furrows his little brow. His thumb presses down on the trigger like his life depends on it. He's told his mum and me he's invented a way of capturing an image, and he's about to find out if he's right.

Every time I look at the photo it annoys me because Marie and I, forgetting ourselves, have got these silly grins on. You know, the faces nobody makes except in photos? You see a lens, and it just feels like the natural thing to do, to offer up the happiest version of yourself for the record. Only for Isaac it's not a record, it's his breakthrough, and we're not meant to have seen a lens before. In the picture I don't see Isaac's sandy springs of hair and his freckles like molecular diagrams. All I see is Marie and I going selfie nearly two centuries prematurely. He was annoyed at how flippantly we'd treated his invention, but Marie reassured him we were just excited at all the wonderful things he was creating for the first time in the known world.

Pinned under the stand of that cheap frame, looking eerily white against the umber of the 'pictograph', is the Discovery Checklist. I've copied the basic design from the Swimming Checklist George Senior made me complete, only instead of Fifteen Metres and Water Skills Two, near the top in my teacher's copperplate hand are written the basic scientific concepts, Gravity sitting just above Force (Centrifugal). The white sheet of paper spills off the desk like a tentacle, line after line marked with the same tick. Where the paper winds under the desk the unticked entries begin – four-ish feet along you've got Magnetism, Radio Waves, Transistors – then it snakes along the floor, around stacks of textbooks and the smell of old leather, coming to rest in the corner by the bamboo plant: Human Genome, Solar Energy, and a few spaces left blank, the ones that really matter. I scan along the list to find the first unticked line, and Electricity sits there, at waist height. Not a bad target for a thirteenth birthday.

I walk across the courtyard to the admin building, and suddenly Pemberton is striding along ahead of me, his young and attractive research students trailing him like ducklings. When the University decided to reshoot their prospectus, guess who was asked to represent the faculty? Professor Universe over there, now available in colour hi-gloss print holding a test-tube up to his blue eyes, now strolling down a corridor with the assurance of a coming epiphany relaxing those broad shoulders, now sitting with a worried student and saying just the right thing to unlock the truth in their hypothesis and simultaneously solve some of their own life problems, thanks Prof Pemberton, I mean Dave, I hope you win the Maxwell Grant For Excellence Brought Into Bloom By Superior Teaching again this year.

To my horror, Pemberton turns, spots me, and in an effortless lecture-hall projection, bellows 'George, hello!' and in four powerful strides, stands before me. As often happens when I'm ambushed, my chat with him is like a lab report of a conversation that happened somewhere else, a bullet-point list of vaguely sensed impressions: the powerful handshake from a firmly-bicep'd arm, a smile revealing coat-white teeth, and a bluff 'You'd be a tremendous help for a journal article old chap, tremendous. Brilliant proofreaders are so hard to find.' I just nod and half-smile and wait for him to stop flaunting his detestable charm.

'How's the boy?' he says.

'Fine. Coming along.'

He pushes a curl of blonde behind his ear.

'Isaac, yes? Always liked the name. You should bring him in one day. He's a genius, I expect.'

Don't grade *me*, Pemberton.

'A chip,' I say, 'off the old block.'

'We must all catch up,' he says. 'Marie too. This month's been so busy.'

'Science waits for no man,' I say, in what I think is a witty parting shot, but as he turns to leave I feel more like I've just ended the conversation on a comma.

{moveable type}

The little circle of oak trees is dense enough to hide a modest family car. I triple-check that the lights are off, spread my brown tarpaulin over my old Astra, and re-lace my brown hiking boots for the trek home. Faraday Cottage is a long walk from the copse and the copse is a long drive from the university, but the precautions are worth it. Marie had a near miss only last winter, when Isaac saw her talking on her mobile phone while coming over the heath, but we managed to convince him she'd been nursing a headache. As we were getting ready for bed in the Secure Area that night I'd wanted to give her a proper ticking off, a real tutorial-style speech about how she'd most of all let herself down, but she reminded me how lucky we'd been to find this place: out of the flight paths, no skyscrapers or power lines in sight, the perfect controlled environment.

'And it's south facing,' she'd said, and dropped off to sleep.

The late September nights draw in fast, so the five o'clock sun makes my shadow stretch far ahead of me as I cross the heath and start hiking down the lip of the bowl. At the rim, the leaves are crunchy underfoot, but the centre still looks like part of a dying summer. Everything climactic seems to pool and linger in the bottom of our valley: sunlight, the departing season, even the cumulonimbus has massed at the heath tonight, threatening to spill over behind me. A badger snout pokes from a hedge, before its owner decides to stay under cover from the possible storm. The bracken has that crunchy, shaven look, bordered by the few flowers that have chosen to cling on to life: crocuses, sternbergia, the shocking pink starbursts of nerines. I snatch a few for Marie, since she's done double shifts as Isaac's lab partner this week and I know keeping up the act can be a strain for her, especially when it's killing week down at her lab.

This is what Isaac Farrow knows:

That he is a thirteen-year-old boy, in a country called England. His father teaches and his mother does something with fruit flies.

That he lives in Faraday Cottage, in a valley, and that while your-mother-and-I have to cross the heath and climb the hills every day to work, there is nothing outside really worth bothering with. That the square of the hypotenuse is the sum of the squares of the other two sides.

That his mother and father love him very much. That love is an evolutionary construct. That we are evolved apes and that, in a way, he's an evolved your-mother-and-I. That the three front doors I'm now unlocking are not to be passed through unless one of us is with him and has checked to say it's okay.

Every time I unlock these doors, check my costume, and step over the threshold, it feels to me like a gift. I'm starting to give him a little more control over what he investigates, and much as I don't like to boast, yes, you *can* reinvent the wheel. His notes are like Leonardo's, only with better handwriting and less philosophy. Philosophy is not on the list. I turn my phone off, double-check by taking out the battery and stuffing both into the secret cupboard, and step through.

The air inside hums with energy — I'm going to have to 'teach' him more about the danger of shocks when I get another mouse from the lab — and my hair stands to attention. Inside, he's using all of his blossoming strength to turn a crank. This makes a sulphur ball spin. In the dark, the ball lets off little crackles of charge. Marie watches appreciatively. Isaac doesn't look up from what he's doing, and while his jaw is set stern his eyes still have the gaze of that two-year-old at the top of the stairs.

'Watch closely, Mum. Dad, don't come any nearer.'

Isaac's voice has the tremolo of puberty; feigned indifference giving way to genuine excitement. I briefly wonder why Isaac should suffer that pretended teen disinterest at all: was that not a Modern thing? Perhaps it's just the way near-adults pretend to themselves they've mastered the world. The coils hum, Isaac and Marie lean forward, and I remember my act.

'Isaac, what's going on? What is this?'

'Dad, the ele-static force I hypothesised this morning? If I'm right, it can cross air.'

I gasp with genuine surprise; Isaac's moving faster than I thought. The housing of the sulphur ball connects, via a long cable, to a tiny tesla coil — a *Farrow coil* — of his own making. The spun metal ring starts to whine, then spark, then there's a flash. An arc of lightning leaps out, burning a jagged line across my vision. I blink a few times but it's still there, bisecting the old workshop with blue light. The flowers in my hand flop over like they've been struck down.

As agreed beforehand, neither Marie or I speak. Everyone has the right to claim what they make.

'Dad, did you see that?' His voice quakes. 'It's a natural force. But it leapt from one place to another.'

I smile. Electricity, tick.

'It certainly did.'

Marie gasps. This is my favourite part of her act.

'But Isaac,' she quavers, 'this changes everything!'

She's rubbing her eyes, shaking her head. I used to think it was a little hammy, but it's Marie that really understands what he's going through, what a breakthrough feels like. We met at a landfill: I was dumping rubbish, she was collecting fruit flies. Her lab, two doors down, was trying to isolate a gene for fast growth; breeding fruit flies, decimating the population to kill the runts, and breeding the survivors again. Every killing week made the sample purer, and the plan was to isolate the winning gene and put it in a vial to sell to agribusiness or fast food or anyone who wanted hypertrophic, hulking produce. At our first department mixer as a couple, Marie joked to Pemberton that she was playing Darwin, a Darwin with earrings, but right now, smiling down at the boy, she looks more like God.

'This force,' she says. 'What are you going to use it for?'

In the gloom, he looks like he's been shocked himself.

'Can't use it for anything. It's dangerous.'

I try to pat his hair down, but it won't stay under control.

'Psh, dangerous,' I say. 'Is dangerous any word for a genius?'

'It could hurt people!'

'In the wrong hands it could, but you never know what you could make with that —'

'No! You don't understand *anything*!' A phrase for the ages.

He pounds up the stairs to his little room and slams the door behind him. Marie looks at my wilted flowers, then at me.

'He's just a boy,' she says, as she does at every birthday. Then, 'When will you have the talk?'

'Oh, that. We did reproduction in the spring. We found a hive of *apis mellifera*, buzzing in a tree.'

She shakes her head.

'Funny. When can we tell him?'

'When he finishes the list, we won't have to. He'll be up to date. Then he'll carry on past the list, and think what he'll do for the world.'

In the dark, framed by a lingering blue glow, my dutiful wife embraces me.

'He keeps asking me about the world. Would it really hurt to tell him a little?'

But this plan isn't mutable. And discovery breeds discovery: that's the beauty of the plan, and the danger of backing out.

This is what Isaac Farrow doesn't know: that every action has an equal and opposite reaction.

{momentum}

Isaac and I are on a very particular barrow, the one we've taken to calling Birthday Hill, and Isaac's tamed the annual campfire with the skill of a woodsman while I watch. I've talked with him about loads of things before in this place: the Coriolis Force, and Minerals and Five A Day. A flock of swallows flew past yesterday, and we talked about migration. Necessary movement. It's still on his mind.

'Where do they go? The African Territories?'

This is one of the disadvantages of having to source historical maps for the boy: he thinks Prussia is still a thing.

'I think so. It's not really my area of teaching.'

'What *is* your area of teaching, Dad?'

How desperately I want to tell him, here and now, ghost stories of nuclei and astrophysics. How he'd love me, hate me. I could tell him of an angry god called Higgs boson, who holds the world together. Would he believe me? I'm not sure what would be worse: if he didn't, or if he did.

'Old, boring things. You're the one who's inventing the future, eh?'

I give him a playful punch in the arm, like I saw Pemberton do once with one of my History Of Science students who was struggling. The girl was so grateful, and I should have been too but I felt like he was demoing an experiment, for my benefit. Isaac smiles up at me in the light from our fire. That hair's darker now, his mother's phenotypes for redness creeping in over the years.

'S'pose so. But why me?'

'You're the genius. That's why your mum and I go off to work every day; so we can get you the things you need for all your experiments. But there's so much more to learn. I expect.'

'Yeah. The other day I was wondering about the way the seeds on the pinecones are arranged…'

I hug him to me, little Isaac, just a head shorter than me, but a head smarter than me. He's gazing into the fire, as you or I might, only he'll be looking for some pattern in how the flames dance, because he's patterned that way, and when he finds it, which he will because he doesn't know failure, he'll want to call it the Farrow Sequence, another thing for the mantelpiece.

'Dad, I reckon everything has an order.'

We're lying on the biggest log, looking up. The embers create a second dusk.

'Very nice theory. How would we test it?'

He points straight up, into space. In the isolation of the bowl, the sky is almost a perfect black, smattered with thousands of stars like spilled flour. Far to the east, a satellite winks and slides away behind some trees. I tense. But he hasn't noticed.

'They do, don't they? The stars. Well, they're not regular, but you do see the same shapes every so often.'

'That's true, well spotted.'

My voice is slipping into lecture, but at the same time this feels like terrific Dad and Son conversation, something he'll recall to me on my death bed and say thanks Dad, without that pivotal moment I certainly wouldn't have become such a rounded and loving human being, plus I wouldn't have discovered Unified Field Theory and similar concepts.

'People have names for them,' I say. 'For instance, over here you can see the —'

'That one looks like a big spoon,' he says. 'The Spoon.'

I wince at the inaccuracy, like Pemberton's just clapped me on the shoulder.

'Yes. In a way, it does... but actually, it's more like a plough.'

'Why should it be? I mean if I look up and I see a spoon, it's a spoon. Isn't it?'

'Yes, but other people call it a plough. You see, they —'

'Hmph. Other people? Well, I've never met them.'

And he's right. He hasn't. And we lie there in silence, under shapes that other people have named, under the sign of Virgo that Marie's secreted copy of *Good Housekeeping* says will make him 'practical, selfless, and earthy', and I have nothing to say to that, or to him, or to what's above us both.

{flight}

'I'm just glad we can have light bulbs now.'

Marie's lilt drifts across the double bed in the Secure Area, mixing with distant storm rumbles.

'He needs to get through resistors and inert gases first, then work out how to combine them. Three, four months?'

In the glow of the candles, her hair's fallen across her face like fine copper wire. If a thousand years of re-enacted science have passed in the thirteen we've slept in this bed together, her smile doesn't show it. The curtains flash with lightning, as the storm spills over the ridge. I think of the way her eyes glowed in the light of Isaac's latest invention, how she's my oldest lab partner. Finally, Little George stirs into life.

'Besides,' I say, 'a candle still has its charm…'

Marie takes off her spectacles, and as we tumble in the crashing storm it's as though nature itself is applauding us for what we're making together.

'Do you remember the first time?'

She's cleaning her lab coat with our secret supply of detergent, a task which always makes her reminisce. The morning light brings out a constellation of fruit fly corpses and brown smears of rotten banana against the rough white fabric.

'Of course,' I say. 'Messy, but it worked. I think.'

That first time, had Isaac been too young to get it? It was Caroline in Neurophysics who'd first talked about how all the geniuses in history, no matter their birth or background, had been given the right access to a few potent experiences early in life. How any child who was conditioned to success would expect it from themselves as an adult. So on the night before Isaac's first birthday, as we were mixing the ink, I steadied myself by imagining I was just testing Caroline's theory. When Isaac woke up, we celebrated his ageing by inventing the printing press with him. Marie presented him with a printed birthday card, illustrated with a rough woodcut of a house martin on the front. We gave him five copies, just to impress upon him the wonder of duplication. I remember his mouth twitching in a smile. I like to think it was because he'd seen the power of technology, but Marie still says it was because house martins are nice.

In the silence of remembering, we realise there's no sound from downstairs. None of Isaac's usual early-morning activity, just the banging of the gate from outside. A gate I most certainly latched and locked in accordance with every precaution Marie and I laid down, that first night when we made all our promises.

I bound down the stairs three at a time, nearly falling into the medieval workshop.

Every invention of the Renaissance is here, but without Isaac amongst them they look like mutations of an original: the weights are imperial, the compass is triangular, the tuning fork has three prongs. Pinned under that tuning fork is a sheet, torn from his notebook. Next to his old Volume Displacement Tables ('Isaac Farrow, Age Six And Three Months') is a note, the ink still damp and shining.

'*Dear Parents,*' in his flowing cursive, '*I spotted my ele-static force in the night! A flash, behind the heath. Have gone to investigate further! Isaac. P.S. Do not be angry. It is for Science.*'

Marie comes downstairs and I show her the note. She just shakes her head. The three front doors are open, my boots are gone from the porch.

Outside, an impenetrable mist has settled in our bowl but there's a faint tramping sound from beyond, in the direction of the University, the direction of staff members glancing sideways at me in the cafeteria, of the local papers pursuing Marie and I, of Pemberton offering a quote: 'Harmless, old George. I'd never have expected this from him.' I stumble without boots, cutting my feet on the unkind bracken, and try a professorial shout ahead of me.

'Isaac! Son!'

But of course, there's no answer to that. Hypothesis?

I'm wheezing like a vice-chancellor by the time the mist thins. The bowl's geography comes into view, rocks worn by nature to trip me up, and beyond that the figure of Isaac. He's bounding across the boulders, and beyond the next ridge is everything he shouldn't see: the motorway over the next hill, the power lines that shunt his electricity across the land by the gigawatt, the tablet screens that make his birthday card look like a flint arrowhead.

A wood pigeon wheels across the sky at full tilt, rushing to whatever flock it calls family. There's a last glimpse of Isaac's back before it moves out of sight behind the ridge, then just the starless sky. A trembling cry of confusion rings around the valley, and I realise that a half-finished list is the least of our problems.

The end of a relationship can also break us apart from our own sense of self, and from our best instincts. In the following story, Kate van der Borgh asks what happens next, and whether it's always possible to reclaim our old identities once the storm has passed.

The History Lesson

Kate van der Borgh

mutter
click
giggle

From her seat near the driver, Alice can hear the usual back-of-the-bus crowd. Snapping, deleting, snapping, uploading. Another shot for Whatsapp, another pout for Instagram, as the breathtaking Neapolitan landscape slides by.

She should tell them to be quiet, to pay attention to the guide, but she doesn't have the energy. Instead she sighs as Mr Kelly, the florid French teacher who smells faintly of mothballs all year round, nods and droops dangerously close to her shoulder.

There's no point looking at her own phone. No new messages. Alice hadn't expected him to get in touch, but she couldn't help hoping. For anything, really: just a few words to say that he's finally done, that he's put the keys through their — her — letterbox. One last text for her to tell her girlfriends about, while they pour the Pinot Grigio and pretend they always thought he was a dick anyway.

She turns to the guide, a young Italian woman who is busy speaking better English than most of the students on the coach:

'The patron saint of Naples is San Gennaro. The people believe he protected the city when Vesuvius erupted and destroyed Pompeii.'

The coach turns sharply and a boy falls ostentatiously into his neighbour.

'Jimmy, you bellend.'

'Can't help it.'

The guide continues, undaunted. 'San Gennaro is famous for the miracle of the blood. A very strange miracle. Three times every year a small container of the saint's blood is carried from the cathedral at Naples to the monastery at Santa Chiara. The faithful come from miles around to pray — and the dried blood turns back to liquid right in front of their eyes.'

Eyes roll, mouths smirk.

The guide continues. 'I know, you do not believe. But this happens almost every year. In fact, when there is no flowing blood, the people of Naples believe bad luck will come. In 1944 there was no blood. That year, Vesuvius erupted and killed twenty-six people. In 1980 there was no blood, and an earthquake in nearby Irpinia killed three thousand.'

Hands rise throughout the coach.

'Where do they keep the blood? In a special fridge?'

'Does it smell?'

As the guide expertly holds the students' fragile interest, Alice leans against her headrest. Naturally, it's too low to rest easily on, too high to snuggle into. Across the aisle, two girls scroll through a selection of photos they've just taken at the summit. Two, or maybe three, photos are of Vesuvius's deadly mouth, gaping in the mist. Fifty are selfies. That's the thing, Alice thinks: you can take these kids to a volcano, a palace, a space station, but they'll still come back with a hundred photos of their own faces.

As she gazes absently into the rear-view mirror, she notices a pair of grey eyes gazing back. She looks away, flustered, fluttering a dog-eared itinerary between her fingers. Don't make eye contact, she tells herself. Not yet, not unless you have to.

She reminds herself that there's only one more day until they're heading back to London, to their crumbling classroom in Walworth. Back to her house in Walnut Tree Walk, and the ruins of her old life.

On the first night of the trip, she had bargained with Mr Kelly: if he patrolled the hotel corridors, intercepting any would-be Romeos and Juliets, she'd take tomorrow's shift.

He agreed, incurious. So she ordered a glass of house white and took it to a quiet spot on the enormous ground floor balcony. From there, she had a view across the coast: scooters wound along mountain tracks, superyachts sparkled just shy of the Sorrento coast. And beyond, looming in the dark, was Vesuvius. Their activity for the final day: a trip up the volcano, and then into Pompeii. Not that the kids gave a shit.

Funnily enough, she'd often dreamed of coming here with Luke. She'd had a turquoise-tinted picture in her mind: her, fresh from the pool, reclining on a wicker chair and sipping an Aperol Spritz. Him, eyes crinkling in the sun, alert to any prowling Italian stallions. Funny, the way we like to see ourselves.

She'd just finished her second drink (both large) when she saw the boy standing there, smiling. She felt caught out, embarrassed about the glass in front of her – was it unprofessional? – but her voice was steady.

'Daniel? You were supposed to be in bed an hour ago.'

He walked towards her, still smiling.

'Sorry Miss,' he said. 'I couldn't sleep. You been out here a while?'

He seemed to be nodding at her wine. She felt her cheeks redden and hated herself for feeling this way – still intimidated, even after a year of teaching. But teenagers are wild, unpredictable.

'You deserve it anyway,' he said, 'what with us lot. We must do your head in.'

And then she laughed, her expression softening. He reached the table and pulled out a chair.

'Do you mind if I just sit here for a bit, Miss?'

'Actually, Daniel...'

'Just for a sec. I wanted to say thanks. For you being good about my mum and dad and stuff.'

So that was it. The divorce was still on his mind. He was a smart, popular student, one of the in-crowd, but things had been tough for him. The boys his age didn't understand what was going on, didn't appreciate how his family life had fallen apart. She knew she could offer wisdom, experience. And, she supposed, a kind of friendship.

'You're welcome, Daniel,' she said.

His smile was broad, disarming. There in the starlight, Alice felt warmed by the wine, and by the trust of this boy – this young man. She felt wanted.

The group picks its way around the ruins. In the heat the girls blot their shiny faces, the boys smell especially ripe. They step quickly through the remains of the spa, past sophisticated carvings and intricate tiling. They cross roads, leaping from one huge stone to another, disbelieving when the guide explains that these are early zebra crossings.

After a while, seeing pale skin turning pink, the guide leads them into a shaded area where tables and shelves are stacked with crockery.

'These are some of the things found in the excavations,' she explains. 'These jars would have been for olive oil, those for wine. Does anybody know why the bottles taper to a point, rather than being flat at the bottom?'

Alice wants to prompt the group, but doesn't know the answer.

'It means you can push the bottle into the earth, hiding it from the sun and keeping the wine cool. The people of Pompeii were very clever, no?'

The students stand, silent. Several have white wires sneaking from under their shirts and into their ears.

Alice shifts in the heat. Her armpits feel sticky, her waistband is tight, and she pulls the stiff material of her suit away from her skin. She moves subtly from one side of the group to the other, putting as much distance between her and Daniel as possible. It's immature, but she just needs to get through the trip. She'll sort things out when they're back home.

Suddenly a girl calls out: 'Eugh! Miss! What's that?'

The group pushes toward a long stone slab. On top, an ash-white figure lies face down, arms outstretched.

The guide nods. Teenagers always come to life at this part. 'I'm glad you asked. This is a cast of a real woman, exactly as she was at the moment Vesuvius exploded and destroyed the city.'

The students whisper:

'Whoa.'

'That's rank.'

'Are those tits?'

Alice shoots a look. 'Ben. Please.'

A boy puts up a hand. 'Does anyone know, like, who she was?'

The guide shakes her head. 'Unfortunately no. She is just one of over fifteen hundred people discovered in the ruins. We know only what we can see today: she was here in the city when the volcano erupted. And, judging by the curve of her belly, she was pregnant.'

The group leans closer. This is more like it.

'Miss?' asks Jodie, one of the quieter students. 'Is she holding her hands up because ash was coming down on her?'

'We think no,' says the guide. 'She would not have been killed by the ash. Scientists believe that, at the moment of the explosion, the temperature here would have reached more than three hundred degrees. So she would have died of thermal shock in an instant. It is likely that the heat twisted and contorted the body after death.'

In the sun, Alice shivers. It's unsettling, this picture from another time. A fragment from a life nobody knows anything about. Who was this woman? Roman? Greek? Cook, seamstress, nurse? What were the true colours behind this lifeless impression? Alice isn't usually sentimental, but she imagines scenes from the woman's life: her, singing loudly and off-key in spite of her husband's gentle teasing. Gossiping about her neighbour's drinking. Combing her elderly mother's hair. What did she see that day when the mountain fumed and raged, more powerful than any god Pompeii had ever dreamed of?

Nobody will ever know. And now she's here, trapped forever in a moment in time: a moment where her future, and the future of everyone around her, stopped dead.

When it happened, she had unfriended Luke straight away. But thanks to their web of mutual friends, it's impossible not to see him on Facebook now and again. That's how, as she sat alone in her hotel room that first night, scrolling through videos of dogs, pictures of food, announcements of engagements, she found herself looking at that familiar face. But this time there was another face too, one she'd never seen before: the one he met a year ago at work, the one that turned his head. The one he'd left Alice in pieces for.

At that moment, she felt as if she was having a panic attack. She threw her phone across the room and slumped onto the carpet, breathing hard. She cried, again, not knowing or caring whether Mr Kelly could hear her from his room next door.

But two, three drinks down — four, counting that shot of vodka from the minibar — as she strolled through the hotel gardens with this softly-spoken young man, the world looked different, brighter. She was only twenty-three, not much older than her students. She had a great job, and she was good at it. And here she was, on this sparkling evening, in the most beautiful town she'd ever visited.

They ambled down a path, shaded by lemon trees. He talked about his friends at home, telling stupid stories, making her laugh. Making her forget about all the shit with Luke, even if only for a short time. She had a sensation of stepping outside her own coiled, aching body, like a snake leaving a shadow of itself in skin.

She stumbled over something, possibly her own feet, and he caught her firmly by the arm; he was tall and strong, like so many of the students his age. The two of them erupted with laughter and immediately shushed each other, conspiratorially. As she righted herself, she felt a swimming in her head. A lightness.

His eyes twinkled. 'Your boyfriend should be here looking after you.'

She heard herself reply: 'I don't have a boyfriend.'

And then they were away from the path. Behind them, beyond a tall hedge, came the sounds of murmuring voices and clinking glasses. But she didn't hear a thing.

While Alice never expected the airport to be a peaceful end to the trip, it's even more head-splitting than their departure from London. From the moment they step into the terminal she's counting heads, dragging students out of chocolate shops and jewellery stores, herding them towards the gate. Mr Kelly is elsewhere, probably sniffing out single malt like a pig hunts truffles.

When they finally arrive at gate 9B, Alice asks the students to call out the numbers they've been using throughout the trip.

'One.'

'Two.'

'Three.'

Daniel is at twelve. She tries to be authoritative as his number comes around but can hardly hold his gaze. She doesn't understand that smile any more: she hopes it's a look of awkward understanding, a tacit acknowledgement that it's all in the past. She knows he's mature enough to understand. But there's something else in his expression, and a crackling in the atmosphere. She feels heat rising, across her chest and up her neck...

There's a click. Alice realises she's stepped in front of an iPhone, held by a fat, freckled student known mainly for his poor hygiene.

'Sorry Matt,' she says, turning. 'I didn't mean to ruin your picture.'

'It's okay,' he says.

Then, as she's walking away:

'I don't mind having pictures of you, miss.'

She stops. What? That was a weird thing to say, wasn't it? The gathered students have gone quiet, and all seem conscious that she's stopped mid-count. Alice wants to ask Matt what he means, but maybe that's just paranoia; maybe he didn't mean anything at all.

There's a rumbling in the distance. It's probably the noise of engines firing. But it feels likes the earth shifting beneath her feet.

Alice feels queasy before the plane has even started moving. She's desperate for a gin and tonic, but she definitely can't get away with it now. Mouth dry, she turns to one of the overpriced guidebooks she bought on the trip and opens it somewhere in the middle.

The book is explaining how the famous Pompeii figures are formed. Turns out they're not preserved bodies, like lots of people think. They're just plaster. Some archaeologist realised that those dead people, buried for centuries beneath the ash and dirt, had rotted completely away, leaving just an empty space in the earth below. By filling the space with plaster, they created ghostly statues of those in their final moments: children sleeping in their beds, dogs straining on their leads. Couples embracing, oblivious.

Alice thinks about this. A moment in time that will last for generations. An impression of a person, made from something that wasn't really them.

And then their lips touched.

In that moment, the world fell away. She became weightless, her body a billion particles scattered on the air.

mutter
click
giggle

As soon as she walks into the office, Alice knows something is very wrong. The headmaster doesn't look up as she takes the chair. He simply sits, jaw clenched, hands folded on his desk.

'Miss Gray,' he says.

Not Alice today, then.

'Yes?'

'We have a problem.'

He slides a pastel-yellow iPhone across the desk, screen side up, as if he's in a cop show or something. Alice takes it. And the last pillars in her world crumble around her.

There's no denying it: her face is toward the camera, while his is nuzzling her neck. Her hands are around his waist. Grasping — you couldn't argue she was pushing. In a moment of quiet shock, Alice finds herself thinking: the zoom on these cameras is really very impressive.

'Miss Gray, you admit that this is a picture of you and Daniel Richardson?'

Of course she does. There's nothing else she can do. At the same time, she doesn't recognise this version of herself, the blank eyes, the wine-stained shirt. In that state she wouldn't have noticed faces hiding behind branches, wouldn't have heard them whispering in the dark.

And yet: thank god this is all they have. Imagine if she hadn't taken him back to her room, if they'd undressed each other right there in the gardens like he'd suggested. Like, she realises now, his friends encouraged him...

The headmaster is saying something about immediate dismissal, about needing to 'contain the situation'. But she knows how this goes. If one student has this photograph, a hundred of them have it. And if it's on their phones, it's on Facebook, Snapchat. It's on the internet. The story could end up with the local press. Hopefully not the nationals, though. Surely not?

But she sees it now: this everlasting clinch, only a Google search away, she first thing a prospective employer will see when they look her up online. Same for any online dates, any potential boyfriends. Is this her history now? There must be laws, there must be ways to force them to take that stuff down…

Back in her flat she doesn't turn on the bedroom light, just takes off her shirt, socks, trousers and climbs completely beneath the sheets. Every so often her phone vibrates in her bag, but she doesn't get up to answer it.

She thinks of what her life used to be. Before all this, she spent every waking moment trying to be the perfect girlfriend to Luke: she went to the gym three times a week, never touched any foods with more than three per cent sugar. She worked hard at her job, and spent her weekends making their home beautiful. Ironically, she hardly ever drank alcohol. Bad for the complexion.

And she never so much as looked at another man. When Luke sees the pictures — as, she realises, he inevitably will — he won't know the woman looking out at him.

But it doesn't even stop there, with the collapse of her reputation and her dignity. Yes, the headmaster, the students, probably the parents now; they know it's bad. But they don't know *how* bad.

They don't know that, on that morning, she'd looked in the bedroom bin, the bathroom bin, hoping that they'd been careful — even though, deep down, she knew they hadn't. They don't know that, for the last few days, she's been trying to blame her feelings of nausea on a bad prawn sandwich. They don't know that her period, famously punctual, is late.

Alice thinks of San Gennaro and his miracle: the magic that means his name will be spoken reverently through the ages. Why can't miracles happen to her? God knows she needs one now. She throws off the covers and goes to the window. In the electric glow of the evening, pedestrians rush in the drizzle, cars streak noiselessly by. She looks for those Sorrento stars, but the light pollution here is too bad and there's only darkness. So she closes her eyes and pictures a talisman many miles away: a crimson vial, held aloft in the candlelight, as voices ask for protection against nature's devastating will.

Placing her hands on her belly, she prays for blood.

When it comes to reputations, a little distance can be no bad thing. The first of a trio of very short stories taken from our 2015 Flash Fiction Competition, 'Beat the Brainbox' won second prize.

Beat the Brainbox

Mike Scott Thomson

'Can the next contestant finally Beat the Brainbox? Find out after the break.'

Camera Four spins to me. I'm spotlighted on the seat of champions, arms folded, smirking.

It's all for show, of course. That's the brief. To diss them, blitz them, then dismiss them. It's a pantomime, but I can't complain. There aren't many jobs where you get paid for answering trivia.

Actually, I'll allow myself to be a little smug. Two seasons in, and nobody's got past me yet. The other Brainboxes have been thwarted a couple of times each. Me: I'm the last man standing,

World Quiz Grandmaster three years on the trot, a fifty-grand bounty on my head. I won't let it go easily.

The commercial break sting plays, and we relax. The studio lights go up. The host has a quick chat with the floor manager whilst I check my Twitter mentions on my iPhone.

'You big mean bully!' someone has posted, with a smiley emoticon. That deserves a retweet.

There's just time to send one of my own.

'You'll need to be a sharper tool than that to beat me!' I type, and press send. Within thirty seconds, it has over a hundred retweets and two hundred and fifty favourites. That's the power of live primetime TV for you.

'Stand by,' calls the floor manager. The studio lights go down and the music starts again.

The host does his thing to camera. From my vantage point, I see the next contestant waiting stage-left: back straight, hands behind back, eyes shut. A concentrator. I don't usually pay much attention to my opponents before their entrance, but this one seems oddly familiar.

'Please welcome the next brave soul to take on the Brainbox, Christos Panayiotou!'

The canned applause plays, the contestant walks on, and now I know it's him.

I first saw it on Twitter. I probably retweeted it at the time, although by that stage it had already gone viral.

A CCTV still: a forgotten corner of a forgotten town, a forgettable workman by a forgettable white van.

Only, it wasn't as forgettable as all that.

The man had been installing bollards: twelve of them, encircling a plaza opposite an office block, ostensibly to stop vehicles driving through.

Before starting work he'd parked his own vehicle in the centre of the plaza. Now there he stood, grasping a large metal wrench, surveying a job well done.

Somehow, the photo got out. Tweeted, Tumblr'd, Facebooked, Reddited, ad infinitum.

'WHAT A SPANNER' read the large white text at the bottom of the image.

When forty-eight-year-old Christos Panayiotou was eventually tracked down and interviewed by a national newspaper, he patiently explained that, no, he hadn't hemmed his van in; those particular bollards were detachable. All it took was one twist of the appropriate tool.

But people would rather believe an unforgettable lie than a forgettable truth.

The host has a quick interview with Christos before we start. He's confident, friendly, smart; he speaks perfect English with only a slight accent. No mention is made of 'Bollardgate', although doubtless social media has picked up on it. I decide not to go there. Instead I stare impassively down – like I do with everyone else – but this time, no dissing. It doesn't feel right.

'... all I want is the chance to prove myself,' says Christos.

'Well, we wish you the best of luck. Let's Beat the Brainbox!' says the host.

The sting plays and we begin.

I get most of them right, as usual. But Christos runs me neck and neck. The single time he gets one wrong, I fail to take advantage and cock up my answer too. The first to twenty has never been so close.

This is no time for pantomime.

I shift in my seat, considering. We all have crosses to bear; many people come on here with their sob stories. But this man was trolled thousands of times, and never once complained. It dawns on me, as we both edge towards the twenty mark, that a troll is precisely what I am. Not only that: I'm being paid for it.

One of these days, my unbeaten record is going to go. So why not control when it happens?

'... nineteen all!' says the host, visibly excited. 'Brainbox, it's your question first. Which term, coined by Richard Dawkins in *The Selfish Gene*, describes "an idea, behaviour, or style that spreads from person to person within a culture"?'

I widen my eyes, letting my character slip. I genuinely don't know. The very fact I don't know has blindsided me. So much for control.

'Trend?' I say at last, but it's a guess.

The host pauses for effect. '*Incorrect.*' He turns. 'Christos, it passes to you. If you know the answer, you've beaten the Brainbox. Think carefully, now.'

Christos's face shows a broad, knowing grin. 'Meme,' he replies.

As triumphant music plays, as the host high-fives the delighted victor, as a glitter bomb bursts from above, I rise to my feet and applaud.

The producer accosts me in the green room afterwards. Never mind the unbeaten record, or the vanished prize pot. He's pissed about something else.

'You were supposed to storm off!'

He's right. The first time I lost, I was meant to throw a hissy fit. 'Oh,' I say. 'Well, I will next time.'

'What do you mean, "next time"?' he says as he walks away.

I shrug and retrieve my iPhone. The first tweet I see is a screenshot of me, wide-eyed and blindsided, taken a few moments ago.

'CAN'T EVEN BEAT THE SPANNER' says the white font.

It's been retweeted over five hundred times. But I can't find any congratulatory messages to Christos.

They must be there, buried amongst the bad. Must be.

I'll be the first to provide one, then.

I put my iPhone away and go find him.

Few losses are felt as keenly as the loss of what we've always taken for granted. It's not easy to cope when we're separated from the certainties of life; like, for example, the regular passing of time. The protagonist of F J Morris's story seems to be coping with the new world in which he finds himself, but will everybody around him? 'Two-timer' won third prize in our 2015 Flash Fiction Competition.

Two-timer

F J Morris

I'm getting out today. I've made it through the programme and into the record books: the first man to have served Idaho's new eighty-year life sentence in nine. Don't get me wrong, I don't want to be remembered for this. But I'm only twenty-nine. I've still got time.

Everyone always asks, what's it like? So I'll be straight up now. Get it out of the way. It's like eighty years has gone, but I don't feel eighty. People don't get that. You won't either. It's like slow motion: a crawl, like being under water. Every day feels like a week, but without being able to sleep half of it away.

To other inmates I'll ham it up, the suffering. People want to hear that it's painful, hard, a huge mindfuck, especially if they're not on the programme. The old-timers, they didn't get the choice like I did. Though there ain't much choice between eighty years and ten. It's a no brainer.

But I've spent every one of those messed-up days, all 29,200 of them, staring at the mountains, thinking about this moment, because there's a load of people outside right now fit to be tied. There are placards and shouting. The usual hatred of humanity loaded and fired at me.

You'll be fine Timmy, everyone said. You betcha. They chose you first 'cause people will be more sympathetic.

It's bull. They're not. I'm an experiment.

You see, I'm serving first degree murder for a felony. Darius was shot by the owner of a house we were raiding. We needed a bit of cash, the house was empty, or so we thought, and although we didn't have a gun, Darius got shot and died at my side. I'm serving time because it wouldn't have happened if I wasn't party to it. The judge threw the book at me. I felt guilty for about sixty-five years. Then I didn't.

I'll bet that half of them out there don't even know what I'm in for. But it doesn't matter. They don't think I've been punished. None of them think I should be allowed to live a full life after taking someone else's. They don't care about rehabilitation, suicide rates, hope for insiders. They don't think that feeling a life sentence is enough. They need a life for a life. There aren't enough eyes to take, or blood to spill. It's not justice they all want, it's revenge. And it isn't revenge for Darius, it's revenge for people I've never even met.

And that's the only word I can think about as I get closer: revenge, revenge, revenge. It ticks down the time that's shrinking back to normal as I walk through the corridors. The minutes pull back together like a snapped elastic waistband. The front desk gives me a hundred dollars and a clear plastic bag with my stuff in it: a packet of chewing gum, clothes, and my watch that's stopped. I unwrap a piece of gum and chew it, but it's soft. I strap on the watch too, more for me than for time keeping. It's hard to stop counting down even when time has stopped.

'Are you ready?' says the guard.

I nod and he walks ahead of me through the front doors, yacking away about something. I hear the roar of voices first. They're all behind the chain-links and razor wire. All the dogs seem to have gone in except for Bongo the Rottweiler. He's on a leash, barking like a hellhound. I can feel the towers watching. The mob, the television crews, and even the Sawtooth mountains are sitting up. I walk towards the car that's waiting to take me away from the front line, but something hits me in the stomach. My mind drifts up like smoke. There's a fog of cheers and screams. People are running, and blood is seeping down my crappy T-shirt.

And all I can think is: man, somebody has good aim.

I fall like an avalanche, grabbing hold of the car bonnet. But I want to see the mountains one last time: the ones serving eternity, the ones who counted down with me. So I push myself around and tumble into the dust, but there they are: the jaw, the green gums, the snow stuck in its teeth, the grimace it's holding for me. I can hear the guard and I can't. His hands push into my stomach but I feel nothing. I look at my watch to count down the seconds, forgetting that it's stopped, and I wait with the mountains, and they see it too, the second hand — it moves.

We don't publish many stories about the creative process: writing is usually at its most powerful when it looks out at the world rather than in at itself. Ren Watson's story about a dramatic schism between creator and created broke this rule and was rewarded with first prize in our 2015 Flash Fiction Competition.

That Buzzing Inside My Head

Ren Watson

I got sick of it one day, that noise in my left ear, sometimes a ring, sometimes a buzz or a hammering sound. I started to poke around in there with one finger, then with the end of my pencil, and then, carefully, with tweezers. That's when I felt it move.

There is nothing worse than knowing there is something alive inside your ear. I started to imagine what it might be: a spider, a fly, or worst of all, a moth. I quickly ran a bath as deep as I could, stripped off and got in. I held my breath, let my head sink to the bottom and held it there.

As my ears filled with water, I felt the thing struggling, and after a while it started to work its way out until I felt it go free at last. I was sure I had felt hundreds of tiny footsteps working their way along my ear canal. But when I lifted my head from the water and looked for the wretched thing, I saw not an insect, but a tiny man struggling in the water. He seemed as though he was sinking, so I scooped him out of the water and laid him on the side of the bath while I got out and hurriedly dried myself and dressed.

We stood there staring at each other a while. I could not really believe what I was seeing. I got close enough to see that he had a tiny pickaxe in one hand, and in the other a birdcage with something inside it which was a vibrant yellow; I can only imagine it was a canary but it was too small to tell.

The noise in my ear had stopped. The man coughed up some water, then he spoke. You might imagine that his voice was high pitched or reedy, but it wasn't. It was just quiet and soft, as though he were speaking to me from somewhere far away. I almost had to hold my breath when he spoke so that I could hear him clearly.

'Let me back in,' he said. 'Let me back in there. There is something I need.'

'What were you doing?' I asked. 'Inside my ear. And what are those for?'

He waved the pickaxe and the birdcage in turn. 'This was for digging, and this to check for poisonous gases.'

'Gases? And digging for what?'

'Never you mind,' he said. 'There's something inside there, and it belongs to me.'

'Inside here?' I said, tapping my head with a finger. No wonder I'd been hearing things. This creature had been digging into my head, probably for weeks. I felt sick. I reached down, pulled the plug in the bathtub and had every intention of flicking him into the water and watching him disappear, but he was ahead of me. He ran. He was like a fly. I could not swat him. He seemed to disappear from underneath my hand every time I brought it down on top of him.

He started shouting at me to let him back in. The voice began to come from all directions, as though he really was flying around the room. It became increasingly desperate; I thought he may cry. I stood very still. I wanted to catch him out.

'I was born in there,' he said in a plaintive voice. 'I grew up in there, it's my home. What's inside there is my birthright, you can't take it away.'

'You know,' I said. 'I can tell you about everything that's inside there. I have it all at my fingertips, with no need for any hard labour. You just have to promise to keep out of my ear.'

I was keeping very still but looking everywhere for him, straining my eyes to try and catch any slight movement that might tell me where he was.

'You're lying,' he said. 'How will I know if you've told me everything, when I can't see it all for myself? You might only tell me half of it, or less.'

Then I felt something tickle my neck and I realised he was there, making his way up, clawing at my skin as though he was climbing a rock face. I felt a tiny hand on my earlobe. I shook my head and then my whole body, in the manner of someone who has just discovered a spider on their clothing. There was a silence then; I knew he had fallen and thought he might be dead, until I heard him cry, 'I am exiled!' The miniature canary flew by me like a speck of dust and disappeared in the glare of the light bulb.

Then he was off again, constantly moving, hiding, advancing on me. I thought of locking him in the bathroom, but he would easily squeeze beneath the door. I would never be able to sleep for fear that he would simply climb back inside me, and get to work once more.

That's when I started running. I ran out of the door and down the street and simply kept going. He followed me. I cannot outrun him. I haven't slept since it happened. Once I took a hotel room for the afternoon, stuffed tissue in my ears and dozed off, but I woke to find him pulling it out, piece by piece, creating a bizarre snow globe scene on my pillow. I am still on the run and now plan to find woodland. It occurred to me that since he is so much like a fly, that there may be some bird or bat that might wish to eat him. The hunter will become the hunted. For now I keep him at heel. When he is gone I will be at peace again, and my thoughts will be forever my own.

In Claire Parkin's story, the division of cells sets off a chain
reaction of further divisions: from mental health to bereavement
to the breakdown in communication between survivors. As
her protagonist discovers, there's only so much you can outrun.
'Splitting Miles' won second place in the 2016 Newcomer Prize.

Splitting Miles

Claire Parkin

Mile One: The Negative Mile

'You're going to take up running,' Beth said. 'So you can do a
sponsored race, in memory of Dad.'

We were coming out of the chapel of rest at the time: stepping
into the crystal light of a blindingly beautiful February morning;
huddled together, blinking, like a pair of dazed crows. Behind us,
I could sense the mourning masses shift and struggle out of their
chairs — desperate to escape, no doubt, a particularly laboured
version of Elgar's *Nimrod*. I loathe *Nimrod*. It was once used in a tea
commercial. Miles never drank tea.

Now this, I told myself, is what happens when you allow your
fifteen-year-old daughter to take on your battered, bereaved self as

her latest project, and you let her get away with it because you know it's the only way she can cope with her own battered, bereaved self. Still, accommodating other people's whims is something I've become really rather good at since that afternoon, just five weeks ago now, when Miles first hurtled through the front door, his pale, round face beaming like a pearl and blethering something about preparing for the arrival of the new Messiah.

'I don't have any trainers,' I told Beth.

'You can borrow mine. We're the same size.'

'And I don't have the necessary, you know, jog-wear. Look, can't we talk about this later?'

'It'll be good for you,' Beth said. 'It'll give you an aim. Recent research suggests that people who exercise regularly have a significantly decreased risk of developing mental illness...'

Gosh, I thought. Who knew? Perhaps, then, we'd have both been spared the agony of your father's psychosis, if only he'd performed a few star-jumps every morning. Oh, Beth, Beth... I know what you're doing and why: that you're groping at bits of research you've read in some crappy women's magazine or other to plug that ice-cold, yawning fear: the one that sliced through the bottom of your belly the instant the policeman opened his mouth to explain what had happened to Dad, and all that spilled from his lips was chaos and the certain knowledge that nothing in your life would ever be certain again.

'Okay,' I said. 'I'll do it.'

'That's my girl!'

And she squeezed my elbow tightly. So much that it hurt a little.

So Beth has bought me a running manual: *The Novice Woman Runner's Handbook* by Mindy Norkman (PhD). She presented it to me at the community centre as we cleaned up after Miles's wake: proffering it in her soft, neat hands while I shovelled the remnants of tinned-salmon sandwiches into the gaping mouth of a black bin-liner. Her timing was lousy: we had just ten minutes to vacate the hall before the Baby-Sing-And-Sign group started at two-thirty sharp.

'Bloody babies,' Beth said. 'I know what sign I'd like to give them.'

She would, too. Beth still has the rawness of an untried adolescent: the rough edge that gets smoothed out after years of rebuffs, rebukes and reminders that speaking your mind isn't always a good thing. She's how I'd like to be if maturity and experience hadn't turned me into a more considerate — or maybe that's more cowardly? — person.

Although the more I think about it, the more I realise that I've never been much like Beth. She's not at all like me or Miles: we are (or in Miles's case, were) short; stocky; cautious. We're rather *grey* people. But Beth is long, lean and quick; everything about her is colour and light. I don't think we ever got over the shock of being handed this red-faced, clamorous baby who was so unlike either of us. Or the surprise we felt at how fiercely we loved her, even though she seemed — still seems — so perfectly alien.

'You'll see,' said Beth, prodding a page with one delicate finger, 'That Mindy splits your training schedule into miles. Mile One — that's The Negative Mile — is where you start. Walking so slowly, you're practically going backwards. There's some psychology in there, too —'

'Oh, super.'

'— Where Mindy explains you'll probably have conflicting feelings about your training. Work through them, though, and you'll move on to Mile Two, the walk/run mile —'

'Where I can intersperse walking with running, building myself up gradually until I'm running full-time,' I said. 'And, no doubt, feeling stronger, mentally and physically, every day. So nothing particularly analogous to the grieving process there, then?'

'I don't understand.' And Beth's face — crumpled, confused — told me she really didn't.

I forget sometimes that Beth is so young. And since Miles, well, stopped being Miles, I suppose I'm guilty of talking to her the way I used to talk to him.

'I'm sorry,' I said. 'I will read the book. Soon, I promise.'

But Beth had turned away from me. A middle-aged man with a heavy, lined face had appeared at the hall entrance: dressed in a creased grey cagoule, with a rucksack strapped to his back and a howling infant clamped to his chest in a sling, he looked like a weary tortoise. How much longer would we be, he wanted to know. Because his back was breaking; he needed a sit-down and his daughter — who was highly sensitive to parental stress — had to settle. I primed myself, bristling for Beth's attack, but it never came. Instead, she stood quite motionless: bin bag clasped against one hip in a tense, pink fist; shoulders squared in her neat black jacket; her long, slim neck unyielding against the rogue wisps of copper hair that had liberated themselves from her topknot and were wafting, jubilantly, around her warm skin.

At last the man made a fluttering gesture of exasperation with his hands before sliding sideways into the toilets, out of sight.

'Wanker,' I heard Beth whisper. 'Stupid, spineless wanker.'

Mile Two: The Walk/Run Mile

This part of north London is beautiful in early spring. The broad avenues of neat, box-hedged Edwardian houses are flanked with cherry blossom trees and the soft pink, quivering blooms swirl through the air with the slightest hint of what Miles used to call 'a mouse's fart of a breeze.' He didn't like the blossom much: the petals stuck to his car's paintwork and would gather — a soggy, brown-pink mass — in the folded arms of his windscreen wipers. Miles was very protective of his car because, I suppose, it protected him. It was the big metal bubble that kept him apart from stuff outside, the same way his microscope kept him apart from stuff at work.

Miles never met the people who owned the tissue samples he examined; never glimpsed the complex, messy worlds that may or may not have imploded, depending on his grading of the microcosm evolving on the slide in front of him. 'All little worlds in their own right,' was how he once described them to me. 'Some ordered and safe; others chaotic and dangerous. All beautiful and miraculous, in their own way.'

Anyway. I've dispensed with Mindy Norkman's advice, and I've leapt straight in with The Walk/Run Mile: I've walked The Negative Mile long enough; I need something purposeful. So today I'm wearing Beth's trainers and one of Miles's sweatshirts. My leggings are too thin, though. You can see the outline of my pants through them, and my buttocks jiggle when I walk. I went into Beth's room before I left and said: 'So, how do I look?'

Beth was rolled up in her duvet, still half asleep. She opened one eye and regarded me dimly. I performed a little twirl.

'Fine,' she said, turning over.

I admit I'd expected more, even at eight o'clock on a Sunday morning: a 'Good luck,' maybe, or a 'Good on you, Mum.'

'Perhaps we can communicate more meaningfully when you're back in the land of the living,' I said. 'By text message if speaking is too much trouble for you, or via Facebook if I'm feeling adventurous.'

'Whatever.'

I was careful to close Beth's bedroom door as noisily as possible.

This is the first time I've walked through Alexandra Park since Miles died. This used to be our favourite route. First just the two of us, then the two of us with Beth: strolling past the deer enclosure; then up through the steep stretch of mushrooming horse-chestnut trees towards the boating lake where shrieking geese, swans, and coots jockey for position on the rippling green water. We'd do one loop then walk towards the sprawling walls and terraces of Alexandra Palace. From here, you can see the whole of London spread out in front of you like a dream; sharp and vivid or shapeless and murky, depending on the day's pollution levels. When I'm alone I like to look at the view through my cupped hands, as though I'm holding whole streets and buildings in my fingers.

I used to work down there, somewhere in all that greyness, in IT. It felt terribly important at the time. And then I had Beth, and she changed me. Or perhaps I was changing anyway and didn't really notice. So I took a job closer to home, less well-paid but safer, helping with the admin and IT at Beth's school. They've been very kind these last few weeks. 'Take whatever time you need,' they said, as if Time itself is mine to take because I'm grieving and for the grieving all the usual laws are suspended.

I've broken into a jog. I feel silly, but it's just me bouncing around on the terrace: the rising, crumbling Palace arches splattered with pigeon shit to my right; London, strangely far away today, to my left.

Strangely far away.

I've remembered something.

Miles, a couple of months ago, sitting at the kitchen table: slowly, thoughtfully, sipping a coffee. I'm sitting beside him. He's popped in briefly, travelling between hospital labs as he often did on a Thursday.

'You seem rather far away today,' I say. It's true: he's barely spoken a word since arriving home.

'Not a good morning,' Miles says gruffly, flicking invisible fluff off his grey suit trousers.

'Oh?'

'Can't say more. Patient confidentiality.'

'But you don't have patients,' I laugh. A stupid, tinkling, vapid laugh, now I look back on it. 'You have samples!'

'I know one of the samples,' he says.

'Really?'

He nods gravely. 'I recognised the name.'

'Oh.'

'The sample is an aggressive oesophageal adenocarcinoma.'

I reach out feebly to touch his elbow. I want to connect, amalgamate; join forces with Miles and this friend, this acquaintance, against such an appalling diagnosis. But Miles's elbow is rigid, poised at an angle as he lifts the cup to his lips. His gulp, as he swallows the last of his coffee, plugs the hollow silence that is forming and expanding between the two of us.

'Poor bastard's had it,' Miles says, easing himself out of his chair and straightening the sleeves of his jacket. 'I'll be back about six.'

He kisses me fleetingly on the top of my head. And then he's gone.

Mile Three: The Endurance Mile

This morning was not good. I shouted at Beth before my run. I told her she was lazy; she called me a selfish cow. It's because I reveal no outward signs of missing or mourning her father. I never loved him, she claims.

No, I told her, it's precisely because I did love him so very much. Ever hurt yourself so badly, Beth, that your body's too shocked, too numb, too wrung-out with screaming inside that there's no source, no substance left to generate any tears? Well, that's me right now. It's all I can do to pump my arms and legs like a loon around Alexandra Park every morning, because that's what you've said you want me to do and I'm doing this for both of us. Pumping, breathing. Pumping, breathing. It's all I can do.

Beth sleeps too much at the moment. All teens sleep a lot, I know, but sleep is all she does. And eat. And fiddle about with her phone. She shuffles about the house, cocooned in her duvet like a surly caterpillar, posting biscuits into her mouth and texting God-knows-who about Christ-knows-what. I should be more understanding, of course. It is the Easter holidays, after all, and only two months since her father died. So what does it matter if her room's a wreck, her laundry's piling up, and her clothes are creased and dirty? I am her mother. Those things are my domain.

But I'm so sick and tired of Mindy Norkman (PhD) and her cod psychology and hackneyed affirmations. 'You're embarking on the Endurance Mile!' she exclaims. 'One mile for mankind, a giant leap for you!' I am ready, apparently, to run a mile non-stop. Just as well, as The Great North London Race is in six weeks' time and, for that, people will sponsor me to run five miles.

'You need to choose your charity,' Beth explained, in a rare moment of sociability. 'MIND, or the National Schizophrenia Fellowship?'

Oh you decide, I said. But your father wouldn't thank you for it. He wasn't mentally ill; he was very firm about that. Miles was never diagnosed, never saw a doctor. Point-blank refused to see a doctor, so convinced was he of the imminent arrival of the Messiah. I was the one who was barmy, apparently, because I just couldn't see it.

And today I can't see much at all. It's been a frosty night and the blast of warmth from the early-morning sun has forced a mist to rise from the melting ground: a shimmering silver film that shrouds the Palace rising ahead of me. I don't like running when I can't see where I'm going.

But we're always running into the unseen, aren't we? And it's just as well. Because if we knew what lay ahead, however would we live? How would we fall in love, bear children, even leave the house each day? Those people who say they can see into the future; they must be fakes or they'd go mad. Why would anyone want to be like that? All that awful knowledge, that crushing responsibility. It must be hell on Earth.

I have run zero point five miles. Mindy's disembodied voice tells me so, blasting from the 'exclusive' *Jogalicious* app that I've downloaded onto my mobile phone. 'Miles run: zero point five. Speed: four point two miles per hour.' Must. Try. Harder.

Life had become hell on Earth for Miles, I think: that's the only explanation for him doing what he did. Though how he ended up in hell in the first place, I just don't know. 'There must have been signs,' people say. 'Things he said or did in the months leading up to him, you know, becoming unwell.'

'No, he was as sane as bootlaces,' I always reply. 'No warnings at all of what was to come.'

But when it did come, it came with a bang, with a crash. And still I go over them again and again: the minutes before Miles burst through the door; those exquisite last moments of ordinariness that, in my head, I can string out for as long as I like. I'm disinfecting the kitchen sink. Rain falls lightly outside. Radio Four babbles in the background, ceasing abruptly with the midday pips.

But then comes a boom of wood against plaster as the front door flies open, striking the wall. And Miles — wild-eyed, euphoric — standing in the kitchen with his arms outstretched.

'For Christ's sake, Miles!' I gasp. 'You scared me half to death!'

'I'm going to be saved!' Miles cries, grasping both my hands. His face is pale and feverish; his pupils dark, dilated. Holes I can't see in to.

'The Lord is coming,' he whispers in my ear. 'I must devote myself entirely.'

'Miles — is this a joke?'

But I know it can't be. Miles isn't one for practical jokes. Miles is a serious man, though has never been — until now — a remotely pious one.

Something seismic is occurring, and I can't understand what it is or where it's come from, or how I can stop the ground from shifting, swaying and splitting beneath the two of us. I'm panicking, but I can't let that show.

'Miles,' I say gently, 'Sit down. Tell me, what's happened?'

'Well,' he says, 'I was driving to work this morning. Faster than I should — I admit — down Long Lane. And then I hit a cat.'

'You hit a cat?'

'Yes,' he says, 'I hit a cat. A great ginger and white thing, appeared from nowhere. So I parked up and walked back to see what I could do. It was in a shocking state: body twisted, blood trickling from its mouth and staining the fur on its chest. Horrible stuff. But strangely, it was purring...'

'Cats do that when they're in crisis, to reassure themselves,' I say, wishing I could do the same.

'So,' Miles says, 'I picked it up. I didn't know what else to do. And I held it in my arms and stroked it, and mopped the blood with my handkerchief. And I kept saying, "I'm sorry, I'm so very sorry..." and still it purred, as if it forgave me in spite of what I'd done. So I closed my eyes and said, "I wish that this had never happened." And then I felt something move in my arms, looked down — and the cat was all right!'

'What do you mean, "All right"?'

'I mean all right — like nothing had happened! No blood, no twisted body. Just a big, vigorous ginger cat purring and squirming and licking my hand! And, imagine this... my handkerchief. *No blood.*'

He produces it from his pocket and waves it in my face, to prove his point.

'And then I heard a voice: half in my head; half outside. All around and inside me! It said: "This is my miracle, the first of many. You — and only you — must prepare for my arrival." So I put the cat down and it rubbed against my legs a bit you know, the way cats do. And I said, "But who are you?" And the voice said, "I am God." and I said, "Well, this is a turn-up. I didn't think I believed in you." And then I looked down — and the cat was gone!'

I've started to weep. Quiet, shuddering, scaredy-cat sobs. Miles puts his arms around me.

'Darling, this is *real*,' he says. 'I promise. Please don't worry. You must have faith.'

I bury my face in his big, crazy chest and start to howl.

Mile Four: The Fartlek Mile

Beth has perked up a bit. I've put her in charge of fundraising: she keeps tabs on my Facebook page and one of those online-donation campaigns.

'Look!' she says. 'I've friended so-and-so for you, you know — that girl you flat-shared with at university.'

And I want to say: 'But I hated her guts, because she always stole my milk.' But I don't. Because this searching and finding; this reconnecting people gives Beth a sense of purpose.

I can run three miles at a stretch now. It's two weeks until race-day, so today I'm Fartleking. That's breaking up your run with minute-long sprints to boost your stamina. Mindy is evangelical about Fartlek, there's even a function on her app for it. 'RUN!' she barks in her peppy Californian accent. And so I do.

It hurts. For sixty searing seconds, my lungs, limbs and heart pump and hammer and howl for relief. Then Mindy bellows 'SLOW DOWN,' and I stumble back into a soothing, rhythmic trot.

I begged Miles to see a doctor. But he was having none of it. He'd smile benevolently, like he thought he was the Pope or something, and produce that stupid handkerchief: first from his trouser pocket, then later — when he'd given up getting dressed in the mornings — from the pocket of his robe.

He'd pace for hours every day. He'd sit in the chair, then get up and strut purposefully to the front door, open it, look out, then shut it and walk back to the chair again. Over and over and over. 'Can you hear it?' he'd say. 'The knocking on the door, the bell ringing. Can you hear it, too? Can you hear the knocking and ringing? Why is He doing it? Why won't He stay?'

RUN!

I'd get very angry with Miles. A terrifying, baffling fury that would whisk me, in seconds, from begging on my knees to threatening him with violence. Just. Stop. Pacing. Just. Stop. Talking. Shit. Just. Come. Back. To. Me. Miles. Please!

I moved out of our bedroom. Miles couldn't sleep — didn't want to sleep — but I craved the oblivion. So I moved into Beth's room where we'd huddle together, shivering, beneath her duvet: Miles padding on the floor below us, thumping out the minutes and hours until we finally fell asleep.

'Why is he doing this?' Beth asked.

'Shhh! Try to rest.'

'Does he hate us, Mum? Is that it?'

'It's a mid-life crisis I think,' I hoped. 'Some men get a mistress or a motorbike, your Dad's just got the Messiah.' And we laughed together like drains.

SLOW DOWN

By the end, Miles didn't have the energy to pace any more. And he'd lost so much weight. He spent that final day in his chair: his grey, shrunken self engulfed in the soft red folds of his towelling robe.

'I need to go out,' I said. 'To the shop, to get some bread.'

Miles looked up at me with a loving smile. 'I'm so, so sorry,' he said.

I stared at him. 'Sorry for what?'

But his eyes had shifted away from mine. He was examining his handkerchief: soiled now after weeks of wringing and handling.

'What a disappointment,' he sighed, shaking his head. 'Such a disappointment.'

RUN!

I wasn't out for long — twenty minutes, maximum. But when I got back, Miles was gone. I phoned the police but they said that other than putting a description out, there wasn't much help they could offer. I didn't know what else to do, so I started making dinner. I got out the vegetables and chopped them up, one by one. I chopped and chopped, and thought of nothing.

The policemen turned up just as Beth arrived home from school. They'd found Miles, they said, and they were sorry but it wasn't good news. He'd been found at Alexandra Palace railway station. It appeared he'd fallen under a train.

SLOW DOWN

AND STOP.

Mile Five: The Finish

I have run four miles now. My legs are rigid with fatigue, and there's a nauseous gnawing in my stomach. But still I propel myself forwards and onwards towards the finishing stretch. 'The crowds will keep you going!' Beth said. But there are no crowds here today: just a few friendly dog-walkers waving encouragement as I and another 499 runners stumble through the early-evening drizzle from Alexandra Park to Highgate Woods and back again.

'Look!' Beth cried just before I left the house, pointing to her laptop. 'Look who I've found for you on Facebook!'

It was the most animated I'd seen her in weeks.

I shuffled closer and peered at the screen. Mindy Norkman (PhD). Posting on my 'wall':

Run!

Run like the wind!

You go, girl!

Run, honey, run!

But then I jerked backwards. Not with disgust at Mindy Norkman's triteness, but because of Beth. I hadn't been quite so physically close to her in a while, I don't know why. We just never seem to spend much time in the same room any more.

And she smelt. The dull, heavy, greasy odour of unwashed skin.

'When was the last time you showered?' I asked.

Beth shrugged. 'Don't know. Does it matter?'

'Possibly,' I said, trying to sound neutral (because, with teens, you should never be confrontational). 'But it would be nice if you could wash yourself before you meet me at the Finish line. Can you do that for me, Beth? Please?'

'Okay.'

'Wish me luck?'

'Good luck.'

I reached out and squeezed her shoulder.

'Bye, then.'

I'm struggling with this final mile. I'm too old, too ill-prepared and nowhere near rested enough.

Miles visited me last night, in a dream. He was sitting in the chair opposite our bed wearing his red towelling robe: arms folded, legs crossed, his face — pale and grave — fixing me with an accusatory eye.

'Why do you insist on splitting me?' he asked.

I propped myself up on my pillows and glared back at him. This, I remember thinking, wasn't how our reunion was meant to be. I felt no tearful relief; no love. I just felt so cross.

'Excuse me,' I said curtly, 'But I think you'll find it was you who split yourself. First, into a broken man I barely recognised, then into dozens of pieces when you threw yourself under that train. If you are referring to the Splitting Miles technique in Mindy Norkman's manual, that is to do with training for the race I'm running in your memory tomorrow.'

'You keep splitting,' Miles said. 'You don't see things entirely. You never did.' And with that he stood up, threw open the curtains and glided out of the open window, into the night.

And I followed him. He wasn't getting away with it again: abandoning us without apology; getting to waft through the dark sky without a care in the world while I panted behind him, demanding explanations. But then I looked down and saw the city beneath us: all bright lights and glinting towers. I heard Miles shout, 'Look!' and so I did.

And I saw him plummet: watched his still, straight body slip through the silent night air; on and on until somewhere, far below, I heard something shatter and saw one of the buildings splinter into thousands of glass fragments. And under each fragment a single red circle was beginning to form: a tiny red-towelling cell that slowly, but very distinctly, was splitting itself in two.

I woke up then. Every part of my body was aching, much as it aches right now. But that was a dream and this is real, and I have reached the Finish at last. I slump over the line, into the arms of a kindly steward who hands me a medal, a cereal bar, and a bottle of mineral water.

I look around for Beth. The other runners have loved-ones all hugging and whooping and high-fiving each other. I feel a pinch of irritation and take a swig of water. Where has she got to? I look at my phone. No text messages. I do, however, have several Facebook notifications. It's a fair bet that Beth's been on it all evening and has messaged me that way instead.

And she has.

I fell asleep. I'm sorry.

And then:

What a disappointment.

I'm such a disappointment.

My hands are shaking so much that I almost drop my phone. I call her mobile. No reply. I leave a message: 'Beth, please call.'

Should I have said something more? 'Beth, I love you. Beth, your messages have put the fear of God in to me. Please Beth, don't do anything stupid. Oh Beth, what have I done?'

Too late now: I have to run. But where? She could be at home; I could go straight there. But what if she's somewhere else? What if she's at the boating lake, wading dreamily into the deep green water? Or on the Palace terrace, biding her time before she leaps down in front of a bus? Or at the station, patiently counting the seconds as she waits on the platform edge?

And how could I have been so blind, so stupid? How could I not see: the oversleeping, the overeating, the not washing, the apathy... Beth's father is dead, and Beth is not coping at all well with the fact. And with all the will in the world, I cannot carry her grief for her, however far I run.

But then I look up and I see her standing on the Palace terrace above: leaning over the railings; her soft, grave face – rounder now than it used to be and leached to a pale grey – blankly surveying the crowd of runners swarming on the grass below.

'Beth!' I shout. 'Wait!'

She looks straight down at me, eyes widening, mouth forming into an O.

'You stay there!' I command, scaling the slippery grass bank. 'You stay right there. I'm coming up.'

She reaches an arm down towards me, grips my hand, eases me up.

'Beth' I whimper, bundling her into me, 'Beth. Don't leave me.'

'Leave you? Why would I leave you?' she asks, pulling away from my arms and scanning my face in puzzled wonderment. 'You're the one who's always running away. Here, sit down.' She points to a bench. 'I brought some juice and Hobnobs.'

'But your messages,' I say. 'You seemed desperate...'

'Yes,' she says. 'I suppose I am. Mum, I'm *stuck*...'

We sit in silence, side by side: Beth leaning into me, her body heavy as stone. I shiver a little, my own body cooling rapidly after my run. But at least the drizzle has moved away and the view of London at dusk, spread out directly in front of us, has taken on a freshness; a startling, brilliant clarity. I put my fingers around my face, the way I do when I'm here alone, so I can hold little tableaux of streets and buildings in my hands.

'What are you doing?' Beth asks.

'Nothing.'

She gently draws my hands from my face.

'Now look,' she says.

And we stay, looking at the view together, for a very long time. Waiting for the darkness to spread across the sky, absorbing the soft red folds of sunset; watching as the breathing city lights beneath us spark and sputter into life.

*If most of the stories in this volume are about the bonds
between people, Anabel Graff's story looks instead at the
connections between ourselves and our memories. 'Soup,
Condensed' won the 2015 Ghost Story Competition.*

Soup, Condensed

Anabel Graff

On our corner on East 95th street, the pear trees had just begun
to bloom, creating a white canopy that looked like heaven. It was
three weeks after my grandfather had died. My grandmother had
just moved into our apartment. I was thirteen.

My grandparents had met in the Brooklyn Navy Yard during
World War Two. My grandmother had been a Rosie the Riveter,
a welder of giant battleships. My grandfather, unable to serve
because of a brush with polio, had been her boss. They met. They
fell in love. They married.

In the weeks following my grandfather's death, my grandmother
insisted on eating nothing but tomato soup, so my mother bought
cans by the crate.

'How come Grandma gets to eat what she wants?' said my little sister Minnie, usually the pickiest eater. (She will eat cooked turkey but not deli turkey, raw tuna but not canned tuna, tomato sauce but not ketchup.) My grandmother brought the thin red liquid to her wrinkled lips. Her face, covered with a soft white down, was as velvety as our hairless cat, Monboddo.

I kicked Minnie under the table. 'Quit it,' I said. Then I whispered so my Grandmother, who was going deaf, wouldn't hear, 'Grandma's depressed.' I had heard my parents say this, but I didn't really understand what it meant.

My grandmother dropped her spoon and said, 'Grandma is a grown woman and if she wants to eat tomato soup, she's going to goddam well eat tomato soup.' She then turned to me. 'Even if she is depressed, don't talk about your grandmother in the third person.' She got up from the table and went over to the pantry. 'I think I'll be eating in my room from now on, Barbara,' she said, untucking her blouse from her pants to make a sling and loading cans upon cans of soup into the polyester. She piled one on top of another until the fabric was stretched to transparency. It was so quiet in the kitchen I thought I could hear the fibres tearing.

'How do you plan to heat it, Ma?' my mother pleaded. 'Should I buy you a hotplate and a spoon and pretend we are on rations like during the war?'

'Don't be ridiculous, Barbara,' my grandmother said. 'I can get my own hotplate.'

I put my hand over my mouth to stifle a giggle.

My mother glared at me. 'Ma,' she said to my grandmother. 'Please, enough with the soup.'

My grandmother turned and took her haul and left the room. We heard her door slam.

'Really, Sarah,' my mother said to me. 'You could show more tact.'

I rolled my eyes and said in a haughty accent, 'If I knew what that meant, Mother, I would try to show it, but I did dress appropriately for dinner.'

This for some reason made Minnie laugh hysterically, and she pointed to our naked cat Monboddo, who had jumped up onto the table to lap my grandmother's abandoned soup. 'Monboddo's tact is showing!' Minnie cried out. Then Minnie and I spent the rest of dinner rolling our eyes and asking if our tact was showing and laughing uncontrollably, which even made my mother smile.

In the hallway outside my grandmother's room I saw a soup can. Assuming it had been dropped during the Great Shirt Convoy of That Night's Dinner, I picked it up. It had duct tape on the bottom but was light as air. I shook it, like I was trying to figure out what my parents had bought me for Christmas, but I couldn't hear anything inside. Underneath, written in red permanent marker in my grandmother's handwriting: BROOKLYN NAVY YARD, 1940.

Minnie was watching cartoons and my parents were talking in the kitchen in hushed voices that I knew I wasn't supposed to hear, so I went into my room to further inspect the can. I took a pen and pried the tape off and released one sticky side. As soon as I lifted up the seal, I felt a pull from my belly button and heard a noise so loud my chest vibrated: the bellow of a ship, hammers clanging metal, yelling, so much yelling. 'Gromney! Clear the dry dock already!' 'Alright! Alright!' in the thickest Brooklyn accents I had ever heard, a lunch whistle, then the sound of a tinny radio and a soft voice crooning: Bing Crosby singing *Only Forever*. I was dizzy, nauseous – the noises so loud

I couldn't see straight — but I managed to smooth the duct tape back over the bottom of the can. My head was pounding, and even though I had been sitting in my room, half my body felt like it had been somewhere else. Then another feeling, of worry — surely my family had heard — so I turned my music on my computer all the way up and peeked my head outside the door but Minnie was still watching TV and my parents were still in the kitchen. My grandmother's door was closed. I wanted to open the can again, but I didn't want to use it all up. It wasn't my sound but my grandmother's.

The next morning, I went to my grandmother's bathroom and saw that the toilet bowl was rimmed in clumps of tomato soup gel, which was disgusting, as was the thought that my grandmother had maybe vomited it up. When I flushed the toilet, it bubbled redder and redder, almost like a science-fair volcano of tomato soup. I was now caught in a dilemma. I should have told my mother that Grandma wasn't eating the soup, wasn't eating anything, but I wanted more sounds.

In the next week, whenever my grandmother left her room, I would sneak in to listen to another can. They were stacked neatly under her bed, hidden from sight. Each one I cracked open and held up to my ear to hear a place far away, a place I had never been, a time in which I had never lived. My favourites: THE DANCE, 1943: a warm sound of saxophones; of feet scuffling in a *slow, slow, quick, quick* rhythm; of swishing crinoline; of two hearts beating in time with the music. OUR WEDDING, 1945: a heavy sound that almost made me cry, not because I was sad, but something else; the expected 'Here Comes the Bride' on an organ, and cheers; and a reprise of the song from the navy yard. BARBARA'S FIRST LAUGH, 1966: a small and bright sound. It lasted only seconds but repeated in short, glorious bursts, and I listened until I was so lightheaded I had to lie down. TEXAS ROAD TRIP 1972: a hot, oppressive wave that grabbed my entire body, as I vibrated with each low of a cow and passing whoosh of a truck. I listened to them all, to the ghosts of my grandmother's forevers, because now they were mine too.

My grandmother's white beard was growing, but the rest of her body was shrivelling. She'd stopped getting soup cans from my mother. If she didn't get more cans, I knew there would be no new sounds.

'Ma,' my mother asked. 'Can't you at least try to sit with us for dinner? It's not good for you to be in your room all day.'

Only I knew that her diminished life was in direct correlation with the increase of soup cans stacked under her bed.

'I am,' my grandmother had said, frowning. 'I'm trying real hard.'

Three months into her stay at our apartment, my grandmother stopped getting out of bed altogether. My parents hired a nurse named Mona to take care of her. I wanted to listen to the soup cans, but her room was rarely empty. One Saturday morning, before Mona arrived or my parents awoke, I snuck into my grandmother's room.

'Who's there?' she asked, but she couldn't see me in the unlit room. Her vision was deteriorating — it showed in the progressively illegible labels on the soup cans. I tried not to make a sound, not to even breathe. 'Minnie? Sarah?' My grandmother was holding a soup can, but this one was barely taped shut. I had left the door open and Monboddo snuck in and hopped up onto my grandmother's bed. 'Stupid cat,' my grandmother said, and tried to push him off, dropping the can, which sang as it hit the floor, rolling towards me. I grabbed it and slid out of the room, because I could hear Mona shaking her keys and saying 'Good morning!'

I clutched the soup can to my chest, anxious for the solitude of my room, anxious for the next sound from my grandmother's life. I knew that these must be the last of her memories. I placed the can to my ear, but I couldn't hear a thing. This one I felt: a warmth, a fuzzy fullness, a tingling. There was no inscription on the label and after a minute, the feeling was gone.

Later that night, I crept into my grandmother's bedroom and whispered in her ear: 'Grandma, what's in the last can? What's the sound that has no sound?' She didn't move. I could see the white hairs on her face, illuminated in the moonlight, her mouth open. I had to resist the urge to shake her awake. I knew that like the soup cans, she would feel empty, light.

The next morning, my parents moved my grandmother to the hospital. A coma. I had been asked to watch Minnie, and as soon as my parents were out the door, I tore into my grandmother's room. The cans were still under the bed. I took one after another and ripped the duct tape off, throwing the soup cans to the floor, adding my own new sound to the cacophony. The Navy Yard, the squeak of my grandfather's leg brace, the sound of Tippi Hedren's scream in *The Birds* at the drive-in in 1963, the lowing of cows from a field outside of Austin, the applause from my mother's first school play in 1975; soon our apartment was shaking with sounds.

Minnie came in with her fingers in her ears. 'What's all this noise?' she asked, scrunching up her nose.

I kept pulling cans out and soon the tins littered the entire bedroom floor. Monboddo chased them around, scrambling every time another one hit the ground. 'Here,' I said, handing Minnie DODGERS GAME, 1947. 'Open it.'

A roar escaped as Minnie threw the can to the ground: hands clapping, cheering, 'Hot dogs! Hot dogs!' and feet stamping and 'Jackie Robinson takes the plate!'

Forty-three cans in all, not counting the unlabelled one that I had in my pocket. And Minnie jumping up and down, clapping her hands, in time, out of time, with the song of my grandmother's soup cans. My grandmother's song played for another hour until we could only make out the slightest buzzing, the vibration of aluminium on hardwood floor. And when the phone rang, and it was my mother, weeping, she didn't have to say a word because we already knew that my grandmother was gone.

Has there ever been a more powerful tool of unity than the Internet? It can strengthen the bonds, or show up the divisions, between people on opposite sides of the world or, in the case of S R Mastrantone's story, between a lonely young couple sharing a home. 'Home Solutions for Mould' won second prize in our 2015 Ghost Story Competition.

Home Solutions for Mould

S R Mastrantone

Martin and I used to talk all the time. Both of us carried around the sort of nervous energy that no amount of exercise or personal projects or sex ever seemed to burn off. Not even Alison, in her teary first three years – those years well-meaning Facebook mums and Facebook dads had made us terrified of – came close to wearing us out. Talking endlessly was our only release, the only way we ever got to sleep at night.

All that went when Alison died. Both the energy and the closeness. We began to orbit one another, with all the vast distance and cold of rocks in space. He'd be at work when I woke up, would come home late and reheat what I'd cooked in the microwave, while I showered and then read in bed. I'd fall into a semi-sleep to the sound of him clacking at the keyboard in the lounge below our bedroom, rarely noticing when he finally joined me at two or three in the morning.

'What do you get up to at night?' I asked once.

'I don't know,' he said. 'Looking for something.'

I wasn't prepared to let us die too. It wasn't fair: like burning down the farm for the sake of a field. We were from a time before Alison, and while Alison brought us immeasurable joy and exciting new purpose, she wasn't meant to be all we were about. Our relationship was better than that.

That was how it began. If our marriage was to stand any chance, I needed to find out what he was thinking, what was happening in his life. And when we stopped talking, I knew I had to rely on other means.

Her funeral was in April. He went from short sentences to one-word-if-I-was-lucky responses in October, specifically around the time Alison would have turned seven.

A new year was underway when I started.

I found his laptop open on the table one morning, switched on but awaiting a password. The bread was in the toaster. The coffee machine was bubbling. On a whim I typed in A-L-I-S-O-N. His home screen came up; the desktop image was of Mount Snowdon.

I didn't snoop then. I was too touched.

The following week I tried going back to work. One of the girls thought it would be a brilliant idea to show photos of her six-year-old's birthday party. They sent me home when I vanished from my desk and was found in one of the toilet cubicles nursing my hand. The doctor was impressed with my Rolando's fracture. She said it was quite rare, although she had come across a few in drunk and hormonal teenage boys who had fancied their chances fighting a brick wall.

I waited downstairs for Martin to come home. He didn't notice the cast on my hand.

In the dark that night, he came to bed but lay on top of the covers. 'How long are we going to do this?' I said. He sighed and said nothing. 'Do you still love me?' I asked.

His response was quick and decisive. He rolled over and placed his hand on my side. Only when he spoke did I realise he'd been crying, his voice was thick and up in his nose. 'God, Jennifer. Don't ask me that. Please.'

'We aren't talking anymore,' I said.

'I just need some time so I can solve this.'

I was signed off again the next morning. I knew it would inspire a bitch-fest in the office. God, her daughter died nearly a year ago, is she going to spend forever off sick? Perhaps they were right.

The laptop was on. This time, once I'd logged in to his account, I opened up the browser. I knew his internet history deleted itself so the toolbar was empty, but I'd recently read an article in which a woman kept tabs her husband's affair by typing random letters into the search box to bring up his previous searches.

I typed in A. After a moment, a small list appeared below my letter at the top right of the screen. My stomach muscles tightened and I looked to the left of the screen. What if I found porn? Or something worse?

Then I looked. *Aston Villa* appeared first. His favourite football team.

I quickly scanned down the list. No *anal sex*, no *Asian hookers*. Instead I saw *Are there beavers in England?* And *aircrash investigation episodes*. I laughed and felt myself relax.

The only thing even slightly unusual in the whole list was: *Are souls real?*

I'm a get-a-little-man-in-the-village-to-do-it sort of person from a long line of get-a-little-man-in-the-village-to-do-it people. My parents had a gardener, an electrician, a cleaner, even a man whose sole purpose was to tend to our gravel drive once a month. Martin isn't a Classic Male in any sense, but his stubborn refusal to pay for help is something straight out of a cartoon from a seventies women's magazine. It's equally funny and infuriating because, as a man of indie-rock persuasion, he isn't naturally gifted when it comes to DIY. He fills in the large gaps in his knowledge by going on internet forums and watching instructional videos.

That's mostly what I discovered looking at his history during the first few weeks. *How do I bleed a radiator? My fridge is too noisy. Fix for condensation on windows.*

He had channelled his grief into home maintenance.

The best was *Home solutions for mould*, to which I applied a metaphorical spin given the stagnant state of our relationship. That was about as insightful as it got.

I checked the radiator, and the fridge, and the windows. They were respectively bled, muted, and dry.

My approach was somewhat random to start with. I'd click letters here and there and hope for the best, often trying out Q and Z due to their good positions on the keyboard, although they were frequent disappointments. Soon I was favouring some letters more than others. W was my absolute favourite. Why this and when that. The Ws filled the entire space the browser allocated to the drop-down list. They were the mother pot and the honey load.

Buried amongst questions about drill bits and garden tools, I found: *What are the side-effects of anti-depressants? What churches are near Blythe? Who is the best philosopher? Why can't I concentrate at work?*

Okay, so they weren't exactly windows into his soul, but to me they showed me he wanted to move forward, showed me he really was searching for this solution. Murky portholes, perhaps?

I had to start keeping a note of all the *W* questions because new, mostly boring, ones would appear overnight, shoving the old ones down the list towards oblivion. Sometimes I couldn't remember which ones I'd already seen and which ones were new.

I tried subtly instigating conversations about my discoveries. 'Do you think the GP would refer us to counselling if we asked?' or 'Maybe if we went out more, to some philosophy lectures, that might be nice.'

'I don't know, my love,' he'd say.

Around the house I left a book about philosophy, leaflets about bereavement and a pamphlet the church had sent through the door. Only the book didn't end up in the bin.

It was approaching February when I was tempted away from the *W*s. The *T* was asking to be pressed. It was just an accident really, a flight of fancy. It wasn't like I was pressing lots of different letters that morning. It wasn't like I wanted my heart broken.

When I saw what was second in the dropdown list, second of four, just behind *tree surgeon in Blythe midlands*, I knew what it was he'd been trying to solve and I started to cry.

Tomboy traits.

At times I had found myself trying to blame Alison for what happened, but that's mostly because I knew what lay down the road of blaming Martin. Mr DIY. Mr A Job's Not Worth Doing If I Can't Do It Myself. Mr I'll Build The Tree House On My Own.

It's not as difficult or monstrous as it sounds either, blaming her, and maybe why my husband was looking up a word that was so frequently employed to describe Alison in lieu of *handful* and *pain in the arse*.

Perhaps if she'd been a little less outdoorsy, a little less adventurous, then she would have stayed inside and played with dolls instead of racking up more cuts and fractures than most people sustain in their whole lives. Perhaps she'd have been safer. And if I'm truthful, what bothered me most was it wasn't a very big step from *Alison's a tomboy*, to *Alison's so like Jennifer*. How many times had that popped up over the years? Friends and family remarking on her energy or her will, the levels of passive-aggression increasing the older and more frustrating she became to them. And how much of a leap then to: perhaps if you'd painted her room pink, perhaps if you'd made her wear her hair long, perhaps if you'd made her aspire to be a fairy princess, then perhaps, just perhaps, she wouldn't have fallen through the floor and broken her neck.

If Martin was trying to blame me, I thought I'd try to be angry about it. Maybe I would try blaming him after all. There was a black harmony in the house with me reciprocating his emotional distance, grunting instead of speaking, walking away when he came to me. From the outside, our orbit must have looked the same as always, but there is a crucial difference when you are no longer just a passive participant.

I even managed to sleep a little bit, something I put down at first to the gradual reduction of Martin's late-night keyboard clacking.

Grudges aren't for me though. I don't have a way to switch off my rational brain. I don't really blame anyone for what happened to Alison, and I didn't really think Martin did. Sometimes there really are such things as accidents, where causes align irrespective of what you did or didn't do. Blame in these cases is nearly big enough on its own to fill the hole left behind when someone dies. It feels substantial, it gives meaning to things, but inside it's hollow.

I'd stopped looking at his searches for a while. When I couldn't hold a grudge any longer, and my insomnia returned, I became curious about his diminishing late night use of the computer. I missed that sound. On some level, even though he couldn't possibly know I was spying on him, I felt we were still communicating. And if we were still communicating, there was a chance we could go back to how it was before.

One morning, around the beginning of March, I logged on to the computer using his password and opened up the browser. The screen was hard to see as early morning sunlight shone through the patio doors that looked out onto the garden. Standing in a dressing gown that probably still had Alison's DNA on it (I doubt I will ever wash it again), waiting for the coffee and the toast, I typed in A. Nothing was there. I typed in S, and H, and Y. Still nothing happened. I moved the laptop into the shade and still saw nothing.

The search history had been erased.

I reached up and pulled the lapels of the dressing gown tighter to my chest. I looked around the kitchen, then out into the garden through the doors, at the giant oak in which a tree house with broken floorboards still stood. The dark eye of its window glared at me so I glared back, both of us accusing the other.

It was me that broke the stare. I went back to the laptop. The letter I looked appealing.

A sentence appeared this time and I drew a long breath.

Is my wife angry with me?

'No,' I said. 'No, I'm not.'

The *D* called out to me from the left of the keyboard, a big grin turned on its side. I pushed it.

Do you acknowledge the anniversary of a death?

'I think you have, my love,' I said.

I did my best to stop the single tear from escaping down my cheek, tilted my head slightly upward and tried to think about something else. It's not crying if the tear never leaves the eye.

It fell when I leaned forward to pull the laptop screen down. I wiped it away with the back of the outstretched hand and went to pull it down again.

W. How could I have forgotten *W*?

I noticed my heart beating faster, like it had risen to the surface to warn me. I pressed *W* anyway.

One sentence appeared in the search bar. Cold spread through my chest and into my belly. I felt my jaw lock my mouth into place and an involuntary moan escaped through the small gap between my lips. I pulled my arm back and folded it over the other defensively, like the words might jump from the screen and bite me.

Why do I see my dead daughter in the garden?

I haven't seen her yet, not properly. The anniversary is next week and so I am hoping I might then. For now I keep watch from the window in the bedroom. It's directly above the patio doors in the kitchen where I now know Martin sits conducting his own vigil.

He doesn't know I know. I went down one night and saw him there, propped up in a dining chair with his back to me, one hand splayed on the glass.

Of course I wonder if I really saw those words on the screen. Time alone can do strange things to your mind. I won't know because he changed the password the day after. But perhaps that password change was indicative of something new, because that night he came home and asked if I wanted to go out to dinner. And we did, and although we barely spoke, when we came back he kissed my cheek before I went upstairs to shower and read and pretend to go to sleep.

Perhaps on the night of the anniversary I will go down and sit with him, but for now I feel close enough. We might be in different rooms yet really we are in the same place now.

Sometimes I think I see something moving in the dark of the tree house, another, darker shadow. It scares me, although I think it shouldn't. When my hand starts trembling I touch the glass and think of all the things Martin and I will talk about once we get started.

Our final story examines the ways in which we go looking
for old connections, still identifying with them and defining
ourselves by them long after they've broken away.

Stay

David Frankel

The sun has fallen behind the ridge, and below him most of the valley is in shadow. If he doesn't find the dog before dark he'll have to give up. Hollins jogs across the uneven ground, but can't keep it up. The turf is wet and uneven and he stumbles frequently as he goes, scanning the gills around him for any sign of the animal. The blood in his hand pumps against the dog's leash, wound tightly around his fingers.

He'd promised Helen it wouldn't get out again. She's never liked him keeping the dog in the shed: 'It's not used to being out there.' But it needs to learn its place. It's never done as it's told, never been any good as a working dog. The boy had spoiled it with kindness. It's like him, always has to be off somewhere, any chance it gets to slip loose. He should've drowned the bloody thing on the day it was abandoned to their care.

Helen speaks about the dog as though their boy will be back one day to collect it, and there is always accusation in her voice: 'You're too hard on it. It's not a farm dog. Don't you ever learn? You leave it in that shed and it'll get out again. You mark my words, it'll go looking.' Whenever she speaks about the dog there is always the accusation of something bigger whispered underneath.

After the boy went there were weeks of shouted words that Hollins can only half remember now; memory obliterated by the white noise of anger. Six months later the police came to the door. A man and a woman, both young, both smart: 'Mr Hollins? Do you mind if we come in?' All the time they were there the dog had skulked in the kitchen doorway, as though it knew. After that, the fighting gave way to long silences.

She'll be home from work by now, in the kitchen of the farmhouse, with its smell of sour bacon fat and dust gathering slowly in corners. They still call it the farmhouse, though it hasn't been a farm for a long time. She'll think the dog is with him, out on the fell.

From the garden gate, he saw it bolt down the lane; a flash of black and white. He knows it came this way, but it is impossible to tell which direction it's gone. He guesses it would follow a route it remembers, the way it used to go with the boy, descending towards the bowl of the valley

As he goes, he whistles and shouts alternately, until repetition turns the sounds into an automatic function that he barely notices. He knows the dog will hear nothing. It will have its nose to the wet ground, the wind in its ears, alert only to the smell of sheep or squirrels.

He begins to think of the moment he'll have to tell her that it has gone, remembering the last time it ran off, how her lip curled downwards, trembling. He'll see the same old accusation in her eyes: 'You promised.' Fucking promises. Fucking animal. As he starts down the hillside it's growing dark. While he scans the landscape, he begins to rehearse the words he'll use to tell her.

Seeing the last of the sun is still lighting the tops of the trees in the valley below, he breaks at intervals into a jog. The darker it gets, the less chance there is of spotting the animal. But it isn't the growing darkness that urges him on now: he's getting closer to the edge of Cramer's land. If the dog makes it as far as the estate, Cramer won't think twice. He's the sort of bastard that keeps his gun by his side, waiting for a chance to use it.

He rarely goes down there these days. He's always preferred the rough heathland on top of the hills. He likes the space, the extremity of the elements. Since his childhood he's navigated the expanses between the rock crags that project like islands from the heather and rough grass. It was something his son never understood: born bored, always straining to get away.

Despite the stinging wind he keeps staring hard into the gloom, his eyes streaming, until almost blind he turns his ankle in a gully. It's only a strain, but it hurts. He limps on as quickly as he can, trying to walk off the pain.

It is slow going until he picks up the rough track that leads down past a barn to the fields in the valley below. It's worth checking. Maybe the dog isn't as stupid as he thought. It might have sensed night coming and taken shelter. The barn isn't old but it is in poor repair. Around it, weeds grow up through rusting farm equipment. Blades that once turned the heavy earth wait to be useful again. The door is shut but not locked. Inside, the soft, sweet smells of agriculture mingle with the reek of diesel and engine oil. On the work bench a few hand tools lie where they were last used, flecked with rust. Their dirty handles look as though they might still hold warmth from the hands that last touched them. The only movement in the barn is a pile of sacks stirred by the breeze from the open door. There is no sign of the dog.

Beyond the barn, ragged fields run towards a wooded area that forms the boundary of Cramer's estate. Hollins scrambles along beside a collapsed wall that follows the edge of a field and, at last, catches sight of the dog. It's trotting along the side of the copse. It stands out briefly in the failing light, a lithe silhouette against a slab of pale rock, before disappearing into the shadows again. He sets off on a course that will intercept the animal at the corner of the wood, before it can reach open farmland, but when he reaches the tree line, there is no sign of it. He doubles back towards the rise where he last saw it.

As he begins back up the slope he sees, at the edge of the wood, Cramer's range rover. It is parked at an angle blocking the track that runs through the trees. Hollins's stomach knots and under his breath he spits the name of his neighbour.

Creeping closer and pushing back branches as he goes, he looks around, desperate to find the dog before Cramer can draw a bead on it. It's darker in the wood, but even in the gloom he can see the bastard is there, standing on the track just ahead. It's too late to dodge him, and maybe it's better not to. Cramer can hardly shoot the dog if he is there with him. At least he can buy time. He steps out of the trees and nods his head almost imperceptibly in greeting. 'Cramer.'

The other man acknowledges him calmly. 'Evening, Hollins. Don't see you down here much these days. You want to be careful sneaking about in the dark. We shoot in these woods. Accidents happen.'

It's difficult to believe that their sons were inseparable, once. Cramer's son helped run the estate now and he'd inherit it all one day.

As usual Cramer, the gentleman farmer, has a broken shotgun under his arm. 'You looking for something?'

Before Hollins can form a reply, Cramer gestures towards the other side of his Range Rover where the dog is sitting, wet and mud-lashed from its travels, with a look of dejected guilt. A thin rope is strung between its collar and the car's bumper. Cramer points roughly with his gun. 'I should shoot it. It's not the first time.'

'It got out. I come lookin' for it, soon as I could.'

'I can't have it running around worrying my livestock.'

Hollins knows all the estate livestock are safely down in the fields at the bottom of the valley, but he stays silent, glowering in the dark as Cramer continues. 'I could shoot it. It'd be quite legal. I'm within my rights. You're a long way from home. What are you and your animal doing running round my bloody woods anyway?'

The two men stand in silence for a moment, the dog whining quietly. Finally, it is Hollins that speaks.

'It goes looking. For him, I mean. It were his dog.' In an effort to stop his words sounding like a plea, he spits them out like a threat. It is too dark for him to see the other man's face properly but he sees Cramer shuffle and lower his gaze.

When Cramer speaks again his voice is softer. 'Well, see you keep it under control from now on.' He unties the rope from the bumper and holds it out to Hollins in a leather-gloved hand.

Hollins takes the dog's tether and yanks it toward him, heading immediately towards the edge of the wood. Face set, he walks up the track that will take him out of the trees into the open ground beyond. Behind him Cramer is saying, 'Can I give you a lift back up to the house? Hollins?' But he keeps walking and doesn't look back. Cramer makes no effort to follow him.

He is tired now and his legs ache. He hates the animal for what it has cost his pride, for the lost hours of work he's spent searching the moor. He hates it for running and for wanting to leave. He pulls the rope hard, and hates the animal even more because of the way it cringes and looks up at him.

As he leaves the track and begins to climb, he can still feel Cramer's eyes on him. Beyond the exposed slopes, a gap in a dry stone wall opens into the narrow lane he has known since childhood. The lane that will take him back to the farm-house. He pauses before going through the gap. At his feet, the dog shivers. It is dark now. The fell has become one deep blue shadow beneath the last pale glimmer of evening. The lane, cut into a deep trough, crosses the hill to the farmhouse where a solitary light shines in the kitchen window: a single sign of human activity that extends neither warmth nor welcome, but makes the stillness of the other rooms solid and their darkness deeper.

He slumps back against the wall, sinking down into the wet grass, and pulls the dog to him. He draws the animal to his chest and wraps his coat around it. Holding it tightly, he presses his head into the soaked fur of the dog's neck and smells on it the mud and brackish water of the fell. Beneath the dog's pelt he can hear the surge of the air filling its lungs and, against his cheek he feels the rapid, vital beating of the dog's heart.

About the Contributors

Kate van der Borgh grew up in Burnley, Lancashire, and left her home town to study music at Cambridge. She then moved to London, where she packed up her bassoon and became a business writer. As well as writing fiction in her spare time, she enjoys opera, trash telly, ghost stories, and worrying about everything.

Alex Clark has had a range of very silly jobs including stonemasonry, archaeology, waitressing, and growing genetically modified plants for scientific research, all of which have been great for material. Her short stories have appeared in collections by The Fiction Desk and Prole. She lives in Cheltenham with her husband and daughter.

David Frankel is a writer and artist. His short stories have been published in anthologies and magazines including Unthology 8, Lightship, and the London Magazine. He has been shortlisted for a number of competitions including The Bath Short Story Award, The Willesden Herald, The Hilary Mantel Short Story Competition, and The Fish Memoir Competition. His MA in creative writing, from Chichester University, was awarded the Kate Betts Memorial Prize. David was born in Salford and now lives in darkest Kent.

Anabel Graff received her BA from Vassar College and her MFA in Creative Writing from Texas State University. She is the winner of the 2014 Prada Feltrinelli Prize and The Fiction Desk's 2015 Ghost Story Competition. Her work has appeared or is forthcoming in Day One, Prada Journal, Joyland, Printer's Row, and The Fiction Desk. She lives in Sag Harbor, New York and is currently at work on her first novel.

S R Mastrantone writes, and spends too much time thinking about dinosaurs, in Oxford. His stories have been published or are forthcoming in Press Start to Play (Vintage / Random House), Lamplight, carte blanche, and Shock Totem. He is a past winner of The Fiction Desk Writer's Award, and placed second in the 2015 Ghost Story Competition. He is working on his first novel.

Hannah Mathewson is a Cambridge-born writer currently living in Norwich. She studied Film & Television at the University of East Anglia, and blogs about writing, depression and her quarter-life crisis for her website ex-aspirational. com. Her debut young adult novel, Strange Weather, will be published as an ebook in summer 2016.

James Mitchell is an advertising strategist and dystopian fiction writer, trying to work out how JG Ballard would respond to Big Data and vaping. His stories have been published in Vice, the Mechanics Institute Review, and Litro, among others. In 2015 he was Highly Commended for the Orwell Society Dystopian Fiction Prize. He tweets at @jamescmitchell.

F J Morris has been listed in a number of competitions, and her stories have featured in a variety of publications in the UK and abroad. These include: Fireworks, Litro's Friday Flash, Popshot, and two National Flash Fiction Day Anthologies. You can find her tweeting at @freya_j_morris.

Claire Parkin worked as a women's-magazine journalist for twenty years (as Claire Williams) before deciding to write fiction full-time. She has been shortlisted twice for the Bridport Prize and is currently working on her first novel. Originally from Wales, she lives in North London with her husband and twin son and daughter. In her spare time, she enjoys reading, running, baking, and sleeping (ideally in that order).

Mike Scott Thomson's short stories have been published by a number of journals and anthologies, including those from Litro, Prole, The Momaya Annual Review, and Stories for Homes (in aid of the housing charity Shelter). 'Me, Robot,' his story to feature in The Fiction Desk anthology Crying Just Like Anybody, was also adapted for performance by the theatre group Berko Speakeasy. Competition successes include the runner up prizes in both the Inktears Short Story Competition (2012) and the Writers' Village International Short Fiction Competition (2013).

Based in Mitcham, Surrey, he works in broadcasting.

Ren Watson is a scientist and short fiction writer. Her work can be found in various places in print and online, and she was shortlisted for the Fish Flash Fiction Prize 2015. She lives in Manchester where she is working on her first collection of short stories.

For more information on the contributors
to this volume, please visit our website:

www.thefictiondesk.com/authors

Also Available

the first nine Fiction Desk anthologies:

1. Various Authors
2. All These Little Worlds
3. The Maginot Line
4. Crying Just Like Anybody
5. Because of What Happened
6. New Ghost Stories
7. There Was Once a Place
8. New Ghost Stories II
9. Long Grey Beard and Glittering Eye

Subscribe

three volumes
for just **£22**

(in the UK, or £29 worldwide).

Subscribing to our anthology series is the best way to keep yourself supplied with the best new short fiction from the UK and abroad. It costs just £22 for three volumes within the UK, or £29 for a worldwide subscription.

(Prices correct at time of going to press, but may change over time; please see website for current pricing.)

www.thefictiondesk.com